Story of
A Foreign Investor

Story of A Foreign Investor

S.K. Uppal

DIVE IN THE OCEAN OF KNOWLEDGE
Ocean Books

Ocean Books Pvt. Ltd.

ISO 9001:2008 Publishers

Published by
Ocean Books (P) Ltd.
4/19 Asaf Ali Road,
New Delhi-110 002 (INDIA)
e-mail: info@oceanbooks.in

ISBN 978-81-8430-272-1
Story of A Foreign Investor
by S.K. Uppal

Edition
First, 2014

Price
Rs. 200.00 (Rs. Two Hundred only)

Printed at
Bhanu Printers, Delhi

To

Taiko

1

The first meeting with the Japanese took place in a hotel. Muni-Lal started thinking if he should wear a suit but the Delhi weather deterred him. A shirt with a tie was his other option, but ultimately the tie was left out. He was not happy with the knot of the tie he chose. It looked a bit big. His shirt and trousers he matched carefully. He patted his bald patch and looked satisfied in the mirror with his general trimness.

He put the car in the parking lot and realized he had nearly 15 minutes to while away. He went to the hotel shopping arcade and saw expensive items—carpets, saris, jewelry and handicrafts. Only foreigners would be buying them, he felt. When he entered the designated coffee house, two Japanese were already there. They politely offered him their name cards and Muni Lal realized that the name of the senior officer was Okada. Other one was Watanabe. The cards were printed in Japanese on one side and English on the other. Muni Lal apologized for not carrying his name cards but offered to show his ID card. It was not necessary, he was told.

"It is very kind of you to have been able to come,"said Okada.

"I am very glad to meet you. As I understand it you are friends of my cousin in Osaka," replied Muni Lal.

"We met Mr. Chaman Lal when we were in Osaka getting Indian visa. The Consul General gave us your name saying that you are a retired senior government official."

"I was in Military accounts. I retired nearly three years ago." Coffee arrived with savories. The Japanese had taken care to order only the vegetarian items. "Have you ever been to Japan?" asked Okada's companion, Watanabe.

"I am afraid not though my cousin has asked us many times. We are a close-knit family."

"India is making great economic progress for 15 years or so. We have decided to set up a plant for manufacturing specialized electronic equipment for automobiles. Indian car industry is growing and parts we make are still imported by India."

"And I must say that our countries have no political problems. Actually, during the Second World War, Netaji Subhas Chandra Bose collaborated with the Japanese with the intention of defeating Britain in South East Asia, of course particularly India. He was born in Orissa where my wife comes from." Okada and Watanabe talked with each other in Japanese. "Let us please have some more coffee," they said and called the waiter.

Muni Lal said, "India was the only country that refused to accept compensation from Japan after the end of the world war." The two Japanese nodded and talked in Japanese. Okada took up the conversation.

"We are new to the county. We already have two contacts in Delhi but we need a senior person like you to help us in dealing with the Government officials. Our impression is that there were always so many people to meet and details to settle." Muni Lal took it as an offer.

"Mostly, it is IAS officers who run the government organizations. I mean Indian Administrative Service Officers. I have a list of all those who joined the service in my year. They also must have retired. The list has their addresses and telephone details. They can have influence."

"That will be very helpful. One of our contacts is a law firm that is helping us to locate a property; I mean land to buy in Haryana state for our plant. The other person is maintaining links in the state government at his level. We will like you to meet the two parties. We will give you a letter officially appointing you as our consultant."

When Muni Lal reached home, his wife gave him a smile. At 60 she had maintained herself well. Her bottom had not extended in a large proportion and the bosom remained fairly tight. She had a grain of mystery remaining in her smile. It was her somewhat darker complexion that made him fall for her after their initial meeting. She waited for him to settle in carrier when time came. She was not mean except, of course, when they did quarrel and also she was aggressive in her views on regional matters. For more than 30 years, the views did not change. She would tell him that cooked carrots were healthy simply because he was disinclined, finding them sweetish even though he ate raw carrots.

"Did you get the job?" Lakshmi asked.

"It was not an interview. They had called me to offer a job and I accepted." "How much will be the payment?"

"Rs. 55,000 per month. I do not have to work everyday."

"Could you not have asked for more?" He was used to her saying that he should have done more. She often told him that his waist was expanding and he should do more exercise. And he would reply that his weight was fairly constant.

He said that if he travelled on the job, they would pay the expenses but Lakshmi pointed out that it was not unexpected.

"Will you have tea?" No, he said he had coffee.

It was the house of a fixed income group man, salaried man. This was all he could afford to build they would say. They did not waste any money. They had only one daughter to marry; Lakshmi was fond of pointing out that there were people even junior to them who had two children studying in foreign universities. How did they afford it on their salary, she wondered? She was intelligent enough to say it in the presence of the right people.

There was an Oriya artifact prominently displayed in the sitting room. The linen had a pattern, somewhat different from the Delhiite. The TV and the music system were Japanese and Korean respectively. The fridge was Dutch and the wife was of the view that it was due for replacement because of age. Both often said defensively that India now manufactured everything and were especially ready to praise cars. But you buy things, may be in a lifetime, only once, so why take chances, they would rationalize.

There was a large bookshelf. There were books on political and economic theories of their university days. When one occasionally talked of selling them, the other mentioned that a second hand bookshop would not purchase them. Will you buy a book that mentioned that Indira Gandhi was the prime minister of India? Nearly a dozen books on chess there lay. They were now rarely opened. Muni Lal purchased them over a few years after joining service but then lost interest. These were works of older Indian novelists like Mulk Raj Anand and R.K. Narayan, obviously the collection of much earlier years. A fine collection of P.D. James was a matter of pride. But the couple's intellectual worth was on display in the works of Gandhi (autobiography), Tagore, Nehru and Dr. Radhakrishnan. They bought fewer books than before but regularly subscribed to an Indian and an American weekly. In bed, after dinner, Muni Lal lovingly grabbed and stroked his wife's buttocks. She turned to him and said, "There was a telephone call from Anju. She and Suresh are planning to come here next month for a week." He played with her nipples. "It is a definite part of Indian culture to consider visit of daughter and son-in-law a great boon."

"We must do something for them."

"We will take them to the zoo and also show a movie."

"Be serious. We should give him a suit and her some gold." Muni Lal took his time to remove his mouth from her bosom."

"Woolens are not available in this season."

"If not readymade, we should give him a good costly piece of cloth." He realized that her underarms needed shaving again. But she was careful to have dusted them with talcum powder.

As a companion, she was a pleasant surprise. As a school boy and even later, he had come to think that men were expected to force women. All the abuses among schoolboys were of molesting other's sisters or mothers. There was no concept of women's participation in sex life. As a boy, he sometimes wondered with his close friends how Sita, a perfect woman, would be willing to have sex with her husband. His experience with Lakshmi was a pleasant revelation. Their relationship was mutual and not without dignity. He learned to respect his wife all his life.

□

2

They lived a quiet life. There were few money problems. As for household shopping, Lakshmi did it for the most part. Muni Lal purchased fruits after some vague understanding that the job belonged to him and also alcohol, though that was an occasional matter. They liked to read the newspaper sharing it in the morning without difficulty. They discussed current affairs moralistically criticizing, without much passion, both the politicians and the government servants. The books they read were not the same, though sometimes they told each other about the content of his or her book.

Muni Lal and Lakshmi both liked to go out for a meal. But discussion would arise about whether they should order drinks with the food. Wife wanted that the drinking could be done at home and it would be cheaper. She also stressed that if they did not order drinks, they could go to faraway restaurants and drive back without trouble. Now they could go to the nearby places only and walk back. Muni Lal said that they could afford a cab occasionally. The discussions were not animated.

Another common interest they had was sightseeing and travelling. They also talked of Muni Lal's colleagues, senior and junior and their wives. They could talk about them humorously and used also strong language. But hidden in his mind were instances of criticism he received, bad postings and losses in competition. His bad memories he could not overcome even when he realized he took his successes as a natural case and that he tended to remember only what had gone wrong. He did not get much satisfaction from talking about these sad matters with Lakshmi sometimes. The help she would give was to say that one had to be lucky with having people of same provincial background, caste and community. His problem of defeats would not go with such consolation. He was not clear what exactly he wanted from her as a result. He felt that the wife had expected him to have greater achievements even though she would ask him not to bother about what looked like his due. Yet they appreciated each other's presence. They missed each other's company when occasional separation occurred.

□

3

The job of the gatekeeper was to keep people out. He asked Muni Lal if he had an appointment with Shri Raghubir Dayal. Muni Lal did not have it but he was not particularly dissatisfied with the situation. The worse would have been to be told that the boss was away. If it were the government office, he would have been told that the Sahib was in an important meeting. He gave his name card and photocopy of the letter of his appointment with the Japanese company and asked that these should be presented to Shri Dayal. In due course, the gatekeeper came back and asked Muni Lal to come in and wait. It was a large area with costly looking sofas. There were three other persons waiting, who discussed some matter with a fair amount of vehemence. Newspapers and magazines were scattered about including a good representation of cinema periodicals. Muni Lal spent some time putting together scattered newspapers but gave it up. When two persons left the chamber, the three men waiting for their turn got up to go in but the messenger called Muni Lal.

"What can I do for you?" asked Dayal who was middle-aged and putting on weight. His name was written on a table name plate to remove any doubt or confusion.

A lady came in and gave Muni Lal a glass of water.

"You have my name card. I am a consultant for a Japanese company called Shin Kansai Corporation, which wants to set up a plant in the Haryana state."

"Yes, I know the company. These people have come to our law firm, Delhi Associates, to help them acquire land for their factory. They need ten acres. They want to manufacture specialized automobile components."

"My contribution can be basically perhaps after the land is obtained. I am a retired government servant, a senior one, if I may say so, who can deal with the state officials. There are naturally many people to meet and documents to bring into being."

"State establishment is not unknown to us. Otherwise, this Japanese company should not have thought us out. We have a reputation. This should be obvious." "What is the situation of acquiring the land?"

"The Japanese company wants a certain number of acres, it wants good road connection, it also wants to be nearer to some companies it will deal with. We are targetting private parties. They may be ready to sell but their agricultural land may not yet be converted for industrial use. They will not admit it. They may even produce fake documents. We, as a law firm, will scrutinize these matters with care."

"Why do the farmers not get the land converted if they have decided to sell?" "You have been a government officer. You should be a man of the world. Conversion process is elaborate, time-consuming and should cost money. The seller will hope that, out of the four buyers, who come to him, one will accept his version, his documents."

"In what way can I help you?

After all, we are working for the same company." "I have put a couple of people in my office in-charge of land acquisition. They will make a list of sites available and then ask the Japanese to look at them. One member of the Japanese company is staying here most of the time. You can go with my man when he is deciding upon the latest position on property. We will not say very much just now. After the land is purchased, legal work like registration will begin. Actually, we are registering the Japanese company in India first. Otherwise no purchase is possible. I hope we can finish acquisition in a month's time."

Dayal called his man Sukhbir and did the introductions. A visit to a number of places along the Delhi-Jaipur road within Haryana was decided upon for the next day.

Sukhbir Yadav drove the car in the morning and Muni Lal sat with him. The car had a small-framed picture of Ganesha and of a saint. Sukhbir looked anxious to talk about Gurgaon. Only 20 years ago this city was just a village. People would come to Delhi on bicycle from here. "Now look at the cars, buildings and hotels," he said. All the impressive tall buildings on both sides of the road were greatly encouraged by foreign investments.

"Where are we going today?" asked Muni Lal.

"To see the sites."

"Have you been there a few times?"

"Yes, yes." There were five sites, three on the left side and two on the other. Sukhbir went to the three, Muni Lal noting that roads and houses deteriorated a great deal after leaving the highway. Sukhbir talked each time about the size of the plot and its advantages. One was well connected with the road, the other was a level area and the third had no known neighbours on two sides.

"Are we going to meet the owners or not?"

"No, not today." said Sukhbir. For the other two plots, they had to go ahead and make a U-turn. 'It was not necessary to see the other two areas,' thought Muni Lal, but even for going back the route Sukhbir maintained had to be followed for some distance.

They went to a well appointed restaurant, known to Sukhbir, for tea. Feeling the questions arising in the consultant's mind, he volunteered information.

"Details of 5 sites, particularly the acreage along with the price quotation are now ready to be given to the Japanese. They can then inspect the places."
"Are they all converted for industrial use?"

"No but we can get it done. The main question is how quickly it can be achieved. Otherwise the rule is there. The forms can be filled up, documents attached and handed over to the designated office. Now you ask officers how long it will take to get the conversion certificate. You will get no reply. The application will be found incomplete, some documents missing. But, at our law firm, we can get it done. The boss is ready to pay money. He will get it back in our own way."

"What about the price negotiation for the land?"

"We have told the seller what to ask. If this price is received, our firm will get a small amount from it from the seller."

"But surely the Japanese can talk to the seller directly. Both buyer and seller can save some money."

"The seller may not be available on a particular day. If he is there, he can't speak English. We will do the interpretation. In any case, he has to quote the price decided upon by us with him."

"Any idea which land will be the Japanese choice?"

"No. But that is not the point. We know which land they should be buying. We will recommend that. If necessary, we will say that three of the five sites are sold out. If they do not hurry, the others will also go and a new round of seeking out land will need to be gone through." Seeing Muni Lal somewhat bothered, Sukhbir ordered another round of tea.

"We need foreign investment," said Muni Lal.

"Our chief ministers are known to go to the developed countries and ask them to come. They are promised all facilities and single-window clearance." Sukhbir considered this thoughtfully. Of course, there are occasions to say idealistic things. There was nothing wrong with Muni Lal doing it. Sukhbir was willing to be friendly.

"The foreign companies have buildings we saw on the way. The Japanese plant, if it comes up, will start making profits in two years or three years. It will recover total investments in a few years flat."

□

4

Mangal Das Joshi was a youngish looking man in middle 30s. Muni Lal was impressed by his punctuality. Joshi was a little corpulent and had a ready smile. He told Lal quickly that he was from East U.P. and also, as if it was a kind of lack of smartness, that he was a strict vegetarian and did not smoke or drink. He gave an impression of being a friendly person wanting to get along.

There was a branch office of the Haryana State government and they were to go there. Joshi said that the boss was a person known to everybody as Kashiji. Joshi had a good relation with him. Joshi could visit him without appointment. He had taken him for lunch to a 5-star hotel. Muni Lal showed no reaction. Kashiji received them cordially. He was fat and had a goatee. Lal found it difficult to mark him down quickly. Joshi neglected to introduce Lal but, when the latter took the job in his own hand Joshi spent time saying what an important retired officer he was. Kashi said that though it was not official or final, yet the date was fixed for the next session of the government allocation of land. This information he insisted was for Joshi only—and then he added for Lal—and that should be kept in mind carefully and confidently. Joshi assured him solemnly. Kashiji explained that there were 8 to 10 officers to hold a meeting and it was not easy to get them together at the same time. A senior man could be called by a minister. There was no escape from it. No time could be fixed definitely for decision to sell government land. The Japanese company should send their proper application to Chandigarh.

When tea was brought in Lal said that he would tell them the difference between a man from Punjab and a man from Haryana. His interest was also to register his importance by not keeping quiet. "Suppose two persons from the states are standing at Red Fort bus station. When the bus comes, the Punjabi would ask the conductor at the door whether the bus would go to India Gate or not". "Nothing will be found written on the bus," said Kashiji to make everybody laugh. Depending on the conductor's reply, the Punjabi will proceed. But the Haryana man will only ask the conductor, "Where will the bus go?" He is secretive. When going, Lal shook hand with the boss and conveyed that Kashiji was a man of the world and was dependable. One could work with him.

Lal and Joshi were still trying to place each other and decided to buy tickets for admission to Jantar Mantar and sat down on the grass. They made no effort to do sightseeing implying that they had known the place. The rate of the admission was negligible. Lal paid but it was much higher for the foreigners. The joke was that people from North-East India sometimes had to show their identity cards to prove being natives.

"I was not born in Delhi but I went to school and college here. It has become such a large city. There are so many new localities", said Lal. Joshi thought of saying something about his background but kept quiet. To keep conversation going he, however, added, "In UP, it is common to say that the city usually has as many colleges as cinema halls."

After waiting for some time, Lal said "If the government makes allocations of land, it must advertise to the clients for them to make applications."

"I do not know about advertisements. There are plenty of applications all the time. The Japanese company is getting itself registered in India for some time through some party. I could have got it done more quickly."

"May be I know the party. They are also trying to get the land from some farmer. Why not get the land from the state government as it will be already converted for industrial use?"

"It is a matter of getting it as fast as possible from any source. The party may be discouraging the Japanese from going for government allotment, saying it would take too much time. Actually applications are dealt with on a first-come-first-served basis. But the foreign party, if it is ready to invest above a certain amount, can be given an out of turn chance to participate in the allotment session. So long as the Japanese are paying the retainership, there is no hurry for their legal party to end discussions with farmers."

"Oh, I am sure things do get settled in due course of time," said Lal trying to overcome certain depression.

□

5

The visit to Chandigarh to hand over application to the state government department. was done by Watanabe and Joshi in one car and by Muni Lal in another, his own. The officer concerned was asked to confirm if the papers were in good order. He would not oblige. He was busy and there were many applicants. He said that the applications were to be scrutinized in due course and those incomplete needed to be rejected. In the evening, the three sat in the bar in the hotel. Joshi did not drink. Muni Lal said that he had not brought his list of batchmates with him. Joshi wondered if there was no way to obtain names and telephone numbers of those who could be living in Chandigarh. He also speculated if it was necessary to come in two cars. He left unsaid that the Japanese company would have to pay Lal's petrol cost. Lal racked his brain how he could make a contribution to the talk. In the noise in the bar, Joshi spoke loudly and authoritatively that he would do something about the application and his favourite god or Deva should not let him be defeated. He would do his best for the payment he received.

In the morning, Rohatgi was present at the breakfast table. He was a young man looking both important and modest. He was new to Lal. Joshi introduced Lal to him saying that the Delhi man was a great government official. Rohatgi said that he was the son of a professor who retired from the University at Chandigarh. He knew all officials, as they were likely to be his father's students. Actually many of them used to come to their house seeking help when his father was teaching. He mentioned names of some senior officials in Delhi whom Rohatgi knew very well. There were also marriage connections. Lal said regrettably but skeptically that he did not know the big names mentioned. Rohatgi assured Watanabe that they should get some satisfaction at the government office that day.

Three of them drove in one car and Lal followed in his own. The officer they had met yesterday did not know Rohatgi or his father. But Rohatgi rattled off a few names and then mentioned where he met these people and also on what social occasions. Ultimately, it was agreed to take out the Japanese application for allotment of the land. The application had some difficult points. One big problem was that the requirement was of a 30-page detailed description of the proposed project and the application had only a 4-page description. Rohatgi asked if an exception could be made in special circumstances. The group was told the official was not competent to make such an exception. They would have to approach the director. Rohatgi collected the names of the director but was told that the director was away on leave or business and that they should go to the superior officer, the joint secretary. What was the time limit during which the application would be made acceptable? 10 days were mentioned.

Rohatgi gave personal reasons for not going to the joint secretary. Back in the hotel, Watanabe called the council of war. Were there any other shortcomings with the application he enquired?

Muni Lal said, "In the government offices, it is customary to take up one thing at a time. What we need is a person who can influence the department to clear our case in toto." It was decided to come back to Delhi to conduct a search for the right person. Joshi said that they were lucky to have Muni Lal, a senior retired officer with them. Muni Lal shook hands with Rohatgi to offer friendship.

On the way back to Delhi after lunch at the hotel in Chandigarh, Muni Lal stopped at the rest house set up by the Haryana government to have tea and snacks. He was in a bad mood. He felt that the imitation western snacks should be banned. He wished he had not ordered snacks. He was witness to interstate buses coming and going and passengers making short stoppages. In a tuck shop, coconuts were smaller than in Delhi but costlier. They must have come from a longer distance. In the university, he fell for an elegant girl, though with small-pox marks. He could not approach her; he felt he had little to offer. Actually, it was not easy for the boys to marry classmates. The boy's career was yet uncertain and was bound to need more time. Muni Lal thought of he and Arti, flying to Switzerland together. Then in a different Avatar, he was playing hockey for India in the Olympic Games. The match was as good as lost but he found an equalizer three minutes before the end of regular time. In extra time, he scored the winner for the hockey team. In Mumbai, a collection of movie stars give the celebration party to the hockey team and he is the obvious star. But he emphasized strongly that they were in a team game.

He started again on the way home.

In Panipat, he saw shops of condiments and handicrafts on both sides of the road and dense mixed traffic. In 1761 or may be 1760, the Maratha fraternity had brought its soldiers and equipment to face invading Ahmad Shah. The battle was fought in January 1761 in north Indian winter. If Maratha forces had won, Muni Lal mused; it could have meant a possibility of escaping British rule. Or was it too late already? In Tarain he remembered, though there was no memorial, of Prithviraj Chohan's defeat by Mohammad Ghori. The Afghan was helped by father of Chohan's wife. But Chohan had earlier eloped with the daughter leading to embarrassment of Jaichand. He had run away with her at her husband choosing (*swayamvar*) ceremony. How many years after marriage was Chohan defeated? In any case the Raiputs had defeated Ghori's army in the first battle of Tarain but he returned next year. It was a broad highway to Delhi now well maintained. In 1857, Sikh and Pathan warriors came down on this way to Delhi to lift the seize of Delhi by the Indian Sepoys and save East India Company's rule.

Do people really suffer as much as depicted in cinema he wondered? The immediate sorrow like immediate touch of fire was what it matters. Gradually people get used to their new condition.

At home as usual not much was said on arrival. When Muni Lal settled down, the wife mentioned that their daughter conveyed the arrival date of the couple. Lakshmi noted that he made no response. She brought tea and asked about visit to Chandigarh, adding that she would like to visit this new city some time herself. Muni Lal said that the job in hand was not easy. There were too many details to tackle. It did not look that even application for allotment of land was going to be accepted.

"You think that a foreign investor was welcome, that the Chief Minister would himself receive him and the beautiful girls of Haryana office would serve tea and delicacies with a smile."

"Go and take a bath" said Lakshmi and removed the things. The door of the bathroom was ajar. Lakshmi went in to switch off the light and removed her clothes and joined him in the bath tub.

"Troubles come and troubles go," she said. Muni Lal realized that she was good at saying little. When they came out and dried themselves, Muni Lal held her from behind. Slowly she extricated herself.

"In the bed," she said.

□

6

Muni Lal and Lakshmi went to the railway station to bring home their daughter Anju and her husband Suresh. At 25, she looked middle aged. Suresh said that she was an excellent cook and an excellent car driver. The parents expressed their gratitude for his appreciation. They were somewhat used to his habit of utilizing the superlative. He had often described various people as "my best friend".

In the evening, Lakshmi told them that she would make North Indian meal and East Indian dessert. Suresh called it an excellent idea. Muni Lal and Suresh sat down to have a drink, while mother and daughter controlled the kitchen. The daughter told about the sad occurrences she had to face from her in-laws. Her husband's sisters took away some of her jewellery. Some items were borrowed for a few days and never returned. She asked her mother if she should ask for them. They shed tears. Mother asked her to take Suresh's help and put her valuables in a Bank. She was also advised not to make anybody angry among her new relations. They kept supplying food to the two men when asked or even unasked, just drying their faces beforehand and looking normal.

Muni Lal had provided whisky of a foreign brand. Suresh said that a new India was producing as good whisky as British. Muni Lal reluctantly agreed and said that everything was available home now. Besides, Suresh said foreign whisky was often fake. Muni Lal said that he had obtained the supply from his friend who has gone abroad and managed to bring 4 or 5 bottles. Suresh said that the duty-free shops do not sell more than 2 to a person but he can buy more quantity from different airports en route.

"Except some Muslim ones," added Suresh to his own strong merriment.

"How are you spending your retirement years? One must continue to work. It is necessary for mind and body. My father used to tell me of a friend, his best friend, and his senior officer full of joy and social life, who felt alone and bereft after ending his job. He began to lose his mind. His memory became poor. He had difficulty in walking. He began to lose his temper."

Muni Lal butted in somewhat hastily.

"I agree with you fully. I have actually been offered a job by a Japanese company. I will give you full details." Realizing that Suresh was reluctant to listen for long, he added "I want to have your advice."

The problem of application for allotment of land that might not be accepted was spelled out.

"What was the way out?"

Suresh said, "Your problem is solved." He asked the ladies to bring them ice and soda and to listen to him. Anju did not know what the issue was.

"I know the most intimate person with the Chief Minister. He is my best friend. He had come to our marriage also. He goes in and out of the CM's office any number of times in the day. When he is not in CM's office, he is in his house. Madan Mohan is the Chief Personal Secretary. He has only to tell the CM and the job is done."

Muni Lal knew that the PS was not a big officer but sometimes such persons had the ear of the superior. In any case, the chief minister would most likely want to have a PS from his own locality and caste.

Suresh was not ready to end his account quickly. He described Madan Mohan's exploits. Yet he was a very discreet person. He would utter no wrong words. Muni Lal asked Suresh if they could go to Chandigarh to meet Madan Mohan. Suresh felt that his father-in-law's request was not put in expressive enough terms.

"Will you like to ring him up and fix an appointment?" asked Muni Lal. Suresh said, "You have not fully grasped the strength of our relationship. If necessary, we can go to his house, we are more than brothers."

Lakshmi asked the men to have one more drink and she would return with her special snacks.

It was decided that four of them would go to Chandigarh. Suresh insisted, well supported by the ladies, that it was an official visit and the cost of petrol and toll taxes would have to be paid by the Japanese. Also room rent at the hotel. Muni Lal said that he could ask for payment of one room rent only and should be paying the other himself. The ladies thought that he was not being aggressive enough. Muni Lal phoned Watanabe to say that he would be off to Chandigarh to settle the application matter and booked two hotel rooms.

Muni Lal got the car ready the next morning. He estimated that 4 hours should be enough from Delhi to Chandigarh. Suresh said that the distance could be done in three and a half. The mother and daughter protested that they needed to make stoppages. Karnal was a source of good eatables. Suresh was of the view that Panipat was preferable.

At Karnal, the women of the house spent time on deciding what to eat. Suresh took the opportunity to speak about his business. He continued it in the car in the later part of the journey. Ludhiana had great export business with Soviet Russia. At least twice a year, their Embassy people would come from Delhi to select quality and quantity of the sweaters, mufflers, socks and blankets the country would import from India. Also shoes. Such a visit was an important event for the industry. The manufacturer worked together, the Hindus and the Sikhs. The entertainment was on a grand scale, though basically it was eating and drinking. The speeches underlined friendship and trust. There was not much talk of communism. Expensive presents were given. After the change of the regime in that country, Indian business fell, perhaps now they buy branded items from France but also cheaper items from China. Now the Ludhiana market is mostly for Indians only. Many new countries have come out of the old Soviet Russia. But business is down. "The Mughal dynasty came from one of these countries if I am right," said Suresh. Now it is heard that prostitutes come from there. The women pretended they had not heard. Suresh wanted to go to Moscow to see if business could be revived. After all, cold weather had not disappeared from there. Muni Lal said that Suresh could go out with one of the delegations. The delegation would not have him, was Suresh's opinion. It was all politics. Muni Lal said that Suresh was young and had so much to look forward to. India was progressing. Lakshmi added that God would give a great deal to a young couple. Suresh maintained that he would take his wife to Russia but Muni Lal made no promise of financing.

□

7

After breakfast, Muni Lal and Suresh went to meet Madan Mohan. They were stopped at the gate of the office. Suresh said that they had come to meet his best friend Madan Mohan but it did not work. After a great deal of pleading, Suresh was permitted to make a telephone call to Madan Mohan. Tension rose as telephone line was busy, but with persistence, Suresh got through. He was told by Madan Mohan that they could not come to his office but visit him at home in the evening. No time was specified.

They returned to the hotel and four of them decided to go sightseeing. Chandigarh was known to be a beautiful city. They had a car but did not know where to go. They sought guidance from the hotel and got a few names of places to go to. The problem of direction remained. The visit to the market was, therefore, decided upon. The mother and the daughter looked at household items, compared prices and had no hesitation to bargain stoutly. For lunch, they managed to go to a restaurant started by a cricketer. Suresh was of the view that the cricketer now had sold it. But his photographs were fixed on the wall.

When the evening came, there was panic because Suresh did not know the home address. But the telephone directory provided by the hotel had the information. It was noted down on a piece of paper but Muni Lal did not want to take a chance. They went by taxi. The house was government accommodation. Madan Mohan was at home. "I have just come," he announced.

"I know how hard you work." Suresh introduced his father-in-law, stating how important a government officer he was before retirement. Then he took over Madan Mohan's case. They were from the same school he mentioned but "Madan Mohan was many years senior to me," he pointed out as a great achievement.

"It is a hard life," claimed Madan Mohan. "I have no time to myself. It is not as if I get special salary. It is only overtime and that has an upper limit. CM is not in town today and that is why I have time to breathe."

"But your special position gives you a unique status," said Muni Lal. Madan Mohan thought of it and did not give a reply but smiled. Children ran in and out of the room, looking happy.

"CM is in Delhi, though this may not be reported in the media. There are certain allegations against him. Please see that this is not to go out of this room."

"Of course, of course," said Suresh.

"This is why I thought it proper that we meet in the house." "Absolutely absolutely," said Suresh.

"What are the allegations? I have not read about them. We read good things about the state, about the progress it has been making. There is said to be much foreign investment,"said Muni Lal.

" The allegations are not by the opposition but members of the ruling party itself or I should say ruling coalition."

"What is the problem?" asked Suresh.

"They are still being kept within the group. But when allegations are made, there is no limit—rape, murder corruption. I am not worried. The headquarters mostly reject such allegations. But some compromise will have to be made. Maybe a member from the opposing group will be installed as a minister." A striking looking girl came with tea items. She was not introduced and she did not greet anybody. When she left. Muni Lal said:

"Your daughter must be in college. You look very young for having grownup children." Madan Mohan smiled, " She is the eldest."

"Do not forget to invite us to her marriage," said Suresh.

"How can it be done without your presence?" replied Madan Mohan, returning politeness for politeness.

"Why have you taken trouble to visit me?" he asked making tea for three. Muni Lal stated, "As Suresh has said, I am advisor to a Japanese company setting up a project in the state."

"Do they pay well?"

"I can say that but it is a temporary job and we have to produce results." "Why have you taken the trouble of visiting my humble abode?" Muni Lal explained how he was anxious to get the application for land acquisition cleared. It was not to be rejected.

"I will be extremely grateful if you could ask the CM to give a direction." "It will not be possible I have to say. CM does not see eye to eye with the Minister of industry. Rumours will start floating that CM took money from a foreign party. Anyhow this is not a job for a minister, much less a chief minister. Officials dealing with investments should manage it."

"But how to approach these officials?" asked Muni Lal.

"Madan Mohan will find a way. He will find a way," Suresh said. Madan Mohan spoke as if talking to himself.

"I have a distant relation retired now. He was in the provincial service but rose well. He should know the director and even the joint secretary of the concerned department. We can ask him."

"The job is done, the job is done," declared Suresh enthusiastically.

"Where does he live?" enquired Muni Lal.

"In Chandigarh."

"Can you please come with us to meet him and introduce us"? Muni Lal wanted to know.

"It is a request."

" This may not be proper," replied Madan Mohan.

"No, no, I agree with you, this will not be proper," Suresh agreed.

"I will be extremely grateful if you telephone him and tell him that we want to visit him."

"You are embarrassing me by your polite expressions." He was in no hurry to phone. He enquired about Muni Lal's carrier. They mentioned the names of officers they could know in common.

As Suresh and his father- in-law did not show inclination to leave, Madan Mohan asked for his notebook of telephone numbers. Contact was made and an appointment fixed for the next morning with assistant commissioner Dayal Singh. Madan Mohan said that they should not praise Dayal Singh's wife for her youthfulness, as it was a second wife.

Next morning, they realized that Dayal Singh lived in an impressive house in a posh locality. "It could not have been built on savings from salary," thought Muni Lal. Then he asked himself not to have negative thoughts. Often these people had land in the countryside, which was sold to invest in towns. There were two garages in the house; one contained a car and the other a buffalo for milk.

Dayal Singh was a tall man with rugged features. He wore a long shirt with pajamas. Muni Lal learned later on that the men in his community did not wear dhoti in public.

Dayal Singh offered them a drink of milk. "I do not believe in tea or coffee." Offer was profusely thanked but refused. Suresh stated, "My father in law was a very senior officer before retirement from government. He is now the special advisor to a Japanese company wanting to set up a plant in the state." "What is the problem?" "The application form for land allotment was quite complicated. It asked for a 30-page description of the project. We have only made a 4-page resume."

"I am not in favour of longwinded official forms. It is not as if 30-page descriptions are read in offices. Even if they care to read, they may not be able to understand. You tell me. I am in favour of looking at the candidate's face and making a decision. I was known to be strict. I got work out of my officers with the use of the stick."

"You are a man with a very impressive background. We request that you may ask the director to clear out application and thus call us for an interview before the board for the allotment of the land."

"I can go and sit in the joint secretary's office and telephone you from there that the work is settled. But this is weekend and I am going to Delhi with the family. Our son has to catch a flight to Canada."

"Can you please ring up one of the officers?"

"No; only face to face."

"If there is anything you will like to suggest?"

Dayal Singh said that the joint secretary, whose name was Satyapalan, played golf. There was a retired brigadier in Dayal Singh's neighbourhood who also played golf. Actually, they were from the same region. Brigadier Vishwanathan could be contacted. "Will south Indians bother about our case?" Muni Lal was doubtful. "They will when I ask." The three of them went to the neighbouring house. The brigadier was out of the house but his wife welcomed them smilingly. She had chiseled-features—narrow arms but wide bottom. She phoned her husband and a meeting was decided upon for the evening. Before leaving Muni Lal asked Dayal if some payment was expected to be done on such occasions. Dayal Singh said that it need not be done in the very beginning.

At the hotel for lunch the women told them that they had gone to a new market area in a taxi. They had asked the hotel to call them a cab. They were told that the charges would be Rs. 500. The women when getting down asked causally what should be the payment and the driver asked for only half the amount. The taxi did not even seem to have a meter. They returned in a three-wheeler scooter. The four of them discussed why the hotel inflated the taxi cost. It could have made the hotel unpopular. Maybe the taxi driver was a relation of the member of the staff. This idea was rejected. There would be many taxies on call. There was some hanky-panky involved was collectively accepted.

"So you are the person who finds fault with our expenses." said Brig. Vishwanathan to Muni Lal in the evening when introduction had been made. There were smiles all around. The Brig. was obviously determined to be friendly. He heard their story and said.

"I do not know anything about investment matters. I will tell Satya what you say."

"Please, also tell him that we are close friends of Dayal Singh."

Vishwanathan contacted Satyapalan. They spoke for a considerable time in their native language. The conversation was not obviously about investment matter only. There appears to be some humorous stories exchanged a couple of times. The Brig. interrupted the talk to check up with Muni Lal some name or detail. Then he announced his verdict that the joint secretary had not seen the papers. And the director was dealing with them. But Satyapalan would speak to him when the office opened about the Japanese company. He would see to it that the proper decision was arrived at. There should be no cause for worry.

Suresh was happier than Muni Lal. Suresh stressed that it was because of his bringing them to Madan Mohan that the work was done. After they are called for interview, the land would be, no doubt, allotted. Muni Lal with a more analytical mind asked Suresh's opinion whether Satyapalan's words were just a promise or actually a commitment. Suresh said that after all so many foreign parties had invested in Haryana. The government was anxious that this should continue. The government servants wanted to clear each case with care and proper scrutiny so that they got no blame for inefficiency. Of course, they might be making some money. Their salaries are low. When the Soviet Embassy people came to Ludhiana, lot of money was spent on entertainment. Muni Lal asked his opinion if he should send a positive report to Watanabe or keep quiet. Suresh was firmly of the opinion that a glowing report should be prepared and dispatched.

He should be seen to be doing things.

They stayed one more night at the hotel. There was no point in starting back late at night. Muni Lal sent a fax message to Watanabe. He said that in Chandigarh he met a number of very important people. It was a busy time for him. Among others one useful person was Dayal Singh, retired assistant commissioner who has given training to the joint secretary Satyapalan. Dayal Singh went to his office and telephoned Muni Lal from there so that with his blessing there should be no cause for worry. Muni Lal copied the fax to Joshi.

Muni Lal spent time detailing his expenditure including petrol cost in Chandigarh. He had the bill for the last dinner in hotel. He found the bill mentioned four guests altogether. He, therefore, reported to the Japanese that Satyapalan and his wife and Dayal Singh were hosted by him.

□

8

In the house in Delhi after the absence of four days, it was necessary to do dusting and cleaning. One electric bulb was not working anymore and another connection was off but that was so for some time already. Mother and daughter developed differences over rearranging furniture. The daughter looked determined; mother said to her that Ludhiana must have taught her interior decoration. Anju said if Lakshmi were to speak to her like that she would not come home ever again and should be considered dead to them. The two husbands settled down to reconcile them but without much success. When the ladies saw the advertisement in the newspaper about the bargain sale, they joined forces again. The daughter sought mother's advice on the dress to choose. Lakshmi stressed that as they were going to the market, they might finish shopping for the young couple also. Suresh said that he did not want anything. The in-laws' blessing was more than enough. Lakshmi stressed that it was not as if the couple was lacking anything but it was parents' duty and pleasure to give them something small and they should not be deprived of their job. The four went off happily.

Muni Lal got a call from Watanabe for a meeting in the evening. Joshi was also there. Watanabe apologized for giving them no advance notice. He said that he was now fairly certain that they would be called for the mandated interview to answer questions about their project and then allotted the land they required. He hoped that they would be given some choice among the available lots to pick up one. Muni Lal said that he had not felt so far that they were approached for any bribes. Joshi acted as if he could say something and would rather not. "Was there anything further to be done besides waiting?" asked Watanabe. Muni Lal assured him that he would keep in touch with the people he had cultivated in Chandigarh. It was not necessary for him to go there again. Letter and fax/phone were available. Muni Lal came away feeling that he had got the better of Joshi.

He prepared a letter for Satyapalan and got it typed in the market. He mentioned that he was the chief advisor of the Japanese company Shin Kansai and a retired senior official. H was in Chandigarh and met Dayal Singh and Brig. Vishwanathan but did not have the opportunity to see Satyapalan. He will not miss seeking a meeting with him the next time.

"It is a great opportunity for the state and for all of us. in Chandigarh. I heard from different sources your great promise for settling investment matters skillfully and expeditiously. The Japanese will not only spend on purchase of land, they will also get construction done, bring machinery and give employment. I look forward to this project coming up soon to join the list of those already having maturity during your tenure. With the kindest regards."

He began to worry if he should end by saying yours sincerely or yours faithfully. He finished by saying yours only. He thought that it was modern or what the students called "cool". He added his name card having name, address telephone and fax numbers. He posted the letter personally.

Muni Lal and Lakshmi drove their daughter and son-in-law to the railway station. There were repeated requests to come again soon. Muni Lal and Lakshmi went to Connaught Place in the evening. It had no recognizable or popular Indian name. Lakshmi and her husband thought at one time that an Indian name would be proper but at another did not want a change. They otherwise agreed that it was proper to remove statues of British rulers from various places. Muni Lal said that it was lucky

Muslim rulers did not erect any statues. "One-fourth of India was Muslim at the time of creation of Partition," Lakshmi pointed out. They were used to the fact that there was little Hindi written regarding shop names, etc. The names of roads were in four languages, namely Hindi, English, Punjabi and Urdu. A shop selling works of Urdu writers had books printed in Devanagari script. It was a specialty shop. At book fairs, a very large number of books were on astrology, numerology and yoga and local medicines mentioned Muni Lal. Lakshmi was aware of her husband's tendency to take a leftist line. She said that if Indian research laboratories invented allopathic medicine, then things could tend to quiet down.

"Now no Indian specialists talked of their products to end TB and typhoid. But there are many advertisements for medicines to regrow hair and end diabetes and cancer and regain vigour. If no sure medicine, just too many offers." They went for coffee. They did it much less often than in younger days. Muni Lal was in the mood of talking about problems.

"Politicians make big money. Even after a few years in power, they become immensely rich with property, gold, even money abroad while they continue to talk of their background of how they did not even have shoes during school days." "There are corrupt politicians elsewhere too. I have read about an African county where the president had more money than the rest of his country put together" said Lakshmi.

"So, we should have that in India also?" asked Muni Lal.

"It will need a lot of calculation," Muni Lal liked her repartees and gave her a smile.

"The poor in India are very poor. The maidservant may get a few hundred rupees a month for being available to work all the time if she got some accommodation and food. When will prosperity percolate down?"

"Why do you not give some more money to the maid?"

"It will only lead to inflation if there is not more productivity. We have foodgrain in godowns being eaten up by rats but not properly distributed."

"Things are improving. My father always talked how prices had gone up in a few years, particularly after the Second World War but never mentioned that pay had also increased. People now have cars, scooters, refrigerators, TV sets."

"It is only a small percentage,"said Muni Lal.

"Look at the people sitting in the café. Most of them are Indians only, a few foreigners. In African big restaurants, it is mostly foreigners." "How do you know?" asked Muni Lal.

"Tell me. Were you making illegal money? Did you know of members of your staff making money?"

"I saw a cartoon once. It is about an office room. One man is saying to another with the big gesture of surprise that there is a man sitting outside who wants to get his certificate without paying us anything. And why do we praise ourselves so much all the time?"

"These discussions were so interesting when we were young," said Lakshmi. She was feeling a little empty at the departure of her daughter.

"If India can only control population," mused Lakshmi.

"It is not done just by availability of contraceptives. People should not only have the means of controlling population but also the willingness. They should realize that they could teach two children better than three. They should be able to see schools, roads, electricity, doctors and mechanization of agriculture. Otherwise might as well have children. Some of them are going to die early in any case." Lakshmi decided to bring him to the subject which was obviously bothering him.

"Why was it..." she asked "that you and Suresh were going on about corruption?" "Let us order something to eat." As Lakshmi took out her glasses and spent time on the menu, Muni Lal marshalled his thoughts.

"This is my first experience of this kind of foreign investment. I am nearing 64. I have to understand matters. All political parties including the communists say that such investment is needed, that it is a good thing. A foreign party applies to get land to set up a factory. Everybody starts saying that money will have to be paid so that you can be considered for allotment."

"It may be only talk. Has somebody asked you?" was Lakshmi's thinking.

"They can declare an application to be defective and tell the candidate to try the next time."

"Did you tie up things during the trip to Chandigarh?"

"I do not know. I hope so." They ate their snacks and drank coffee in silence.

They resumed conversation on different matters.

"We should have a programme of doing things like visiting monuments, there being so many historical monuments in Delhi or visiting well known markets," suggested Muni Lal.

"We should go on weekdays and not holidays. Also we should plan a trip outside Delhi We have not gone out by ourselves for quite some time."

"There is the question of the Japanese projects. Let the details get settled."

The good news arrived at last and the letter from Chandigarh came in Muni Lal's name. The group in Delhi had been hearing rumours that such letters had already been received by others. They felt helpless. The letter was of an official nature from a director. The signature was there but no decipherable name. It said that on scrutiny the application for allotment of land for setting up the project by Shin Kansai Corp in the state was found acceptable. The original owner or members of the company concerned should present themselves along with their representatives, if any, for an interview with the Allotment Board. The date of the interview would be conveyed in due course of time. The receipt of the letter should be acknowledged.

Muni Lal faxed the copies of the letter to Watanabe and Joshi. He got a telephone call from the former expressing his happiness and asking that the acknowledgement letter may be sent. He suggested that they should meet and have a drink together.

When the three of them got together after two days, the question was how long will it take for the meeting for the interview to be convenient and how they should prepare themselves. Watanabe said that he was in touch with Osaka and it was not likely that somebody else would come to the meeting. He then asked for what they would like to have and said that he was, of course, aware that Joshi did not drink and was a vegetarian. It was agreed that there was no point in ordering scotch at the bar. They were not likely to get the genuine stuff. So, it was Indian whisky or beer or gin.

"Indian rum was also quite good," Joshi said. He did not want to be excluded from the talk.

"As regards how long should it take before the meeting in Chandigarh, I have already started making enquiry. I am not given to falling into inaction. As soon as our application was cleared, I contacted Rohatgi in Chandigarh. He said that generally it took a month. Many senior officers were involved and they should be given sufficient advance notice. As for the preparation for the interview, I have also not been inactive. I have instructed Rohatgi to find out who are the persons who would be present in the allotment board and then we will contact who we can in advance to know what questions are to be faced." Joshi felt he had regained his importance.

"Rohatgi should be properly paid," said Muni Lal. Joshi made a small gesture implying that this had been already taken care of and Muni Lal should not bother. "The candidates are given only four or five days notice. Sometime the meeting is postponed." Muni Lal said that if there was free time he would like to go out of Delhi for a few days with his wife. It should be altogether five days' absence. He would leave his contact address. This was agreed. Muni Lal and Joshi came out together but the latter went in from the door saying he has forgotten to convey something to Watanabe.

□

9

It was a happy period for Muni Lal and Lakshmi. They spent time sitting together working out where to go for a few days. They came to a conclusion that it would be a hill station. This was an off-season. Holiday season was over and winter had not set in yet. Hotels were advertising in newspapers that discounts were available. For the couple, it was more of a job to decide what to choose. They went over a number of places looking at positive and negative factors. One station had developed a dubious reputation of having a severe shortage of water. "But this problem was in summer," they corrected themselves." "It was to be Manali," they decided. They had not heard much about it except that it was an apple exporting area. Muni Lal took out his old book on tourism. It had names of hotels, their tariff and telephone numbers. His basic aim was to find out from the hotels their rate and deductions they were offering.

The telephone numbers did not work. Obviously the numbers had changed. They decided to go to a big office complex in Janpath. It had many tourism offices among other set-ups. The first place they tried did not help. People were busy talking on telephone. At last, a person attended to them but cut them short by pointing out that the office dealt with hotels owned by the state only. The second place was helpful. Rates of various places were made available. Muni Lal enquired about off-season concessions. The shop checked these up obligingly on telephone from two places and said that they would get 15% off. The couple was fairly close to making a decision when they learned that the distance from Janpath to Manali was about 580 kms. Muni Lal did not want to do it in one day. They would also have to make a couple of stoppages. Lakshmi did not drive. They said that they might travel one day at leisure and stop the night in Chandigarh.

The tourism shop fixed them up to leave after two days and provided them some pamphlets. Tea had arrived in the meantime. Was the rate higher through the shop than if they had gone directly to the hotel? 'No' the shop assured them. It was actually lower. The shop got a payment from the hotel for bringing clients.

Now that they were stopping for a night on the way, it was not necessary to start early in the morning. They were both serious about maintaining physical cleanliness. Muni Lal was happy that he was to leave only after shave and bath. They took out some woolens but told each other that it was to be a casual affair. No neck ties for him. Car was topped up, petrol being costlier outside Delhi. They tried to work out humorously how much saving it was going to amount to.

They left after breakfast and stopped in Kurukshetra for lunch at a rest house set up by the state. Haryana prided itself on these places on main roads. They came out after lunch to see the city famous for the battle between the Pandavas and the Kauravas in which Lord Krishna played a crucial part. It was not exactly history as no firm dates were available. But religious people said that the earth in Kurukshetra was red even today from the amount of bloodshed in the battle. The Information Office was ready with printed material but there were no guides that the couple could hire. So, which way to go? What to ask for? Lakshmi asked a scooter driver if he would kindly tell them which road to take towards the battleground. They got a blank stare. But followed general directions of going left from the Gurudwara and continuing onwards for the big water tank or lake. They managed to reach the temple situated where it was claimed Lord Krishna had given the message of the Bhagavad Gita. The shop nearby sold statues of Lord Krishna and DVDs of the Gita with the English or Hindi translation.

Eatable stands and beggars established it as the proper site. They removed their shoes—there were policemen nearby to protect them - and entered.

It was a largish compound. There was a statue of Lord Krishna with a round net surrounding. There was an ancient tree nearby. They quietly moved about. "So much time has passed," said Lakshmi.

Muni Lal said to a watchman, "Armies of the Mahabharata must have been spread all around."

"Yes, from here to Jind."

"Is there a place connected with death of Duryodhana as it would mean the end of the 18 days of warfare."

"Yes, there is a tank with a temple near it." He seemed to like talking about the ancient fighting.

"There was a rule of fighting. At the sunset, fighting ended everyday. The warrior would untie the strings at one end of his bow. Shri Krishna found out ways to finishing the big Kaurava fighters but never going against the rules."

"We will like to go to the tank and the temple you mentioned. Can you please find somebody to show us the way? We have a car." The watchman managed to find them an urchin. He sat with the driver and Lakshmi shifted to the back. The tank was deep. There were steps going down to it from different directions. But the water was low and dirty. A priest kept telling people without being asked specifically that Duryodhana tried to hide in the tank but was challenged by Bhima and came out.

"How deep do you think is the water?" murmured Lakshmi.

"In the rainy season, this tank must get filled," said Muni Lal. The priest thought it might be a tricky question by Lakshmi.

"For those who come here, what matters is the devotion in the heart." At the temple, there were framed pictures of the five Pandavas. A group of women wearing south Indian saris was throwing marigolds at the pictures. The priest was back. "People who come here with pure heart go to Heaven."

Somebody asked the priest to describe Duryodhana's fight with Bhima. He was willing to oblige. Duryodhana was also very brave and skillful in fight. Before the last encounter, he went to see his mother Gandhari. She asked him to remove his clothes. Though she always covered her eyes with a piece of cloth to act blind, Duryodhna felt hesitant to remove his underwear. His mother through her Yogic power made his body impenetrable to weapons but his thighs which were covered remained like that of any other human being. Bhima hit him there. It proved the priest said that evil would have a bad end.

Muni Lal and Lakshmi tipped the guide and got into the car to get out of the town. He said

"Kurukshetra was more about Lord Krishna, the philosopher and a man of action unlike Mathura where he is dealt with as a child and a youth. In Mathura, there are many stories difficult to accept. In Mathura, I was told that Nanda, the foster father of the Lord Krishna, had 7 lakh cows, the number neither increasing nor decreasing obviously. If you go on a boat on the river Yamuna, the guide will tell you that Yamuna happened to be a sister of Yama, the god of death."

"There are mythological stories. Let us not forget positive aspects. The Mahabharata is a great book. Some people may be distorting some aspects, some parts of it."

The two were in agreement on Indian matters, though tended to take up opposite sides to go over a subject matter. She was generally skeptical but when it came to matters concerning her background, concerning the great Rath Yatra in Puri or Mahaprabhu Chaitanya, who lived in Orissa she was not to be countered. These were matters of culture to her.

"When something is a matter of culture in India, you can't do anything about it," said Muni Lal.

"Is giving bribes also a matter of culture?" Muni Lal looked at her to see what mood she was in.

"Well," he responded, "somebody will say that he was honest but he had sisters to marry off. His father passed away and left the responsibility on his shoulders. He has to now develop means of income in whatever way possible."

"There is one thing,"came out Lakshmi with some deliberation.

"Depending on the group orientation whether people around you tend to be more religious or more academic, they will talk of after-lives ending in heaven or on assimilation with Brahma."

"It is a matter of belief. Every community follows some belief. We at least do not kill those who disagree with us."

"On the one hand, we talk of all in one, and, on the other, maintain such strong discriminations based on caste."

"It is going away slowly," said Muni Lal.

"But talking of afterlife, there is a story I heard from a lady. She had gone to an astrologer shortly after marriage. He was very positive. She and her husband were together in their previous lives also. They would be together in their next life also. Then she would achieve salvation after a happy and noble existence. The story made me think that clever people like astrologers know that people are not terribly keen to be disconnected with the world. Not very soon."

The two of them had sometimes thought of hitting out, attacking or casting off but mostly found a compromise.

They reached their hotel in Chandigarh before sunset. After a little rest, they went to the bar. Lakshmi also agreed to have her occasional drink. The bar was very loud with full blast music going and they moved as far as possible from the source of music to be able to hear each other without shouting.

"We have been married for 36 years," said Muni Lal.

"Is there any sequence to this statement of fact?"

"There was so much more I wanted to do for you."

"We have not wasted money." They had differences at the time of Anju's marriage. Lakshmi wanted to spend more than the husband but it was over now. She was anxious to escape his entering into self-depreciating stories. But she also had her bouts to depression. A word even from him at a time would make her angry or sad while on another it would leave no impact.

□

10

They had a little difficulty getting out of Chandigarh on road to Ropar. They asked a few times and once were sent to the direction opposite to the correct one.

The hill road started shortly after clearing Chandigarh. Muni Lal said that going to Mussoorie from Dehra Dun might mean 40 kilometers of hill road or less but here they were faced with 240 kms. Lakshmi moved from side to side constantly. At lunch at a hotel, they did not take risks and opted for toast and coffee. There had to choose between dhabas and hotel-restaurants. There were plenty of dhabas mostly claiming proudly to be pure vegetarian. Lakshmi said that they were being vegetarian was possibly due to problem of maintaining meat properly in the dhaba- a great north Indian invention of roadside eateries- particularly in summer. They passed the main towns on the way namely Bilaspur, Sundernagar, Mandi on the well-maintained road. At the outskirts of Kullu, they felt relief.

But Kullu turned out to be a problem. It was crowded in the evening. In the main road, there was miscellaneous traffic and quite filled it up. It was tiring feeling fairly near, yet being becalmed. It took something like an hour to get to the other side of Kullu. The more impressive shops seemed to have imported items. Kullu's specialty was shawls. The road to Manali was quite wide and not so circuitous as could be expected. The hotel was on the main road. The hotel had advertised that all rooms faced the Beas river. Actually, the river accompanied the road much before Kullu even. From the hotel room, it could not be seen at night. The hotel had also advertised free drinks on arrival but they were not there. But it was a good hotel with modern equipment. Muni Lal told the bellboy that the hotel looked quite new. The local chap agreed and said that Manali had 1,200 hotels, big and small. They all agreed that it was a town, which had really grown big. The food was a mixture of Indian and western but mostly Indian.

The morning was bright. Lakshmi opened the curtains and the narrow swift flowing river was very much there. Also on view were massive mountains some covered with snow. The breakfast was buffet mostly north Indian but with some south items and toast and omelet. As for fruits the hotel had not gone beyond banana and papaya.

By 10 a.m. Muni-Lal and Lakshmi were ready to go out. Some drivers washing cars were consulted and they suggested that a guide should be hired, as they being outsiders would not know what road to follow. The boy that was acquired sat with Muni Lal in front. He suggested the first place to go should be the Hadimba temple. The description in front of the temple, possibly provided by the Archeological Survey of India, described the temple to have been built by a king some 500 years ago. Hadimba is now considered a goddess but was actually of a Rakshasa ancestry. But with prayer and devotion, she became a good person. She had a brother who was very brave. Hadimba said that she would marry only that person who could defeat the brother. In due course, Pandvas came along. Bhima fought with Hadimba's brother and killed him. Hadimba married Bhima and they had a son. In the Mahabharata war the son fought with Karna who had to use his special- and only one in number - weapon. Therefore when Karna faced Arjuna he did not have his special weapon.

Lakshmi said to Muni Lal that Karna's ratha got stuck in mud, he got down to extricate it. Arjuna killed him on Krishna's advice even when Karna had no weapon in hand, an attack that could be a violation of the rules of war.

The wooden temple had beautiful carved doors and planks. People offered money out of devotion.

Muni Lal and Lakshmi went to the side to take photographs. Seeing the camera, two women came with rabbits with them and offered that rabbits should be held in hands by one and photographed by the other for Rs. 10. They were getting many customers. A little way off in a quieter place, two men came one after the other and offered to sell an aphrodisiac to Muni Lal.

The next place decided upon to visit was Rohtang Pass. This was an important place to reach from Manali because generally hill stations do not have too many interesting places to go to. They basically provide cool weather in summers and also good scenery. Rohtang was an alternative route to Kashmir besides the more familiar way through Pathankot and Jammu. The guide announced that it was 52 kilometers away. It was a narrow road cut into mountain ranges. It was not as high as the road to Khardungla in Ladakh. But even in this comparatively cut off place, habitation seemed to be springing up. There must have been a good deal of crowd of tourists in summers. The guide said that local people used their private cars as taxies in summers. Now the road was quieter. They looked for snow. It was October and sunny but in a few secluded spots, snow survived from the last fall. It was not cold. At Marhi, some 10 km or so from Rohtang they were stopped by some semi-professional persons. They were not permitted to go any further. There was construction work going on. Officers sweetened the prohibition by saying that in any case the cars would not have managed to go further because of the road condition. And they should consider themselves lucky to have come thus far as they could have been turned back earlier. Lakshmi took some photos. They joked about trying to cover the remaining distance on mules. Muni Lal said laughingly if some bribe should be offered. He asked the senior man what they should be doing now to go further. They had come all the way from Delhi. He replied like a good bureaucrat that they should get a written permission from his superior officer without specifying where to find him.

"You look very sexy in dark glasses," Muni Lal told Lakshmi.

"When is it that I do not do so?"

They stopped in the main market in the city of Manali to look for a restaurant. It was lunch time. There were Tibetan, Punjabi and mixed offerings of food from various regions. Gujarati food was commonly advertised, showing that people from there were good travellers. Muni Lal and Lakshmi decided to return to the hotel.

The next moment they felt they were running out of the sightseeing places. They decided to do some walking. A well-established hotel claimed to be pure vegetarian and offered 'typically' Gujarati, Punjabi and South Indian fares. They walked along the river. There was no walking avenue. The river was quite a few meters below the road and full of some big stones and numerous small ones. People were throwing their garbage from the road into the riverside below. There were accumulating plastic items, bottles, food containers. Potato harvest was being packed in an open wide corner near the river.

"There should be many garbage boxes in the town. We have not seen any," said Muni Lal.

"After that, step one, people should use these garbage containers. Step two, they should be regularly emptied by garbage trucks belonging to the municipality and, step three collected items should be burned or buried in agreed upon locations." Muni Lal gave his wife an appreciative look.

They got into the car and went to the main market near the Mall or more commonly known as Mall road. There were similar Mall roads in Shimla and in Mussoorie, they knew. But separating from the main market were small narrow lanes offering merchandise. The contrast between the few big streets and the small lanes was striking. There was a similar situation in the hill stations they had been to – Shimla, Mussoorie and Nainital. Perhaps these houses along the narrow lanes were what these towns had initially till the British and later on tourism opened up these places. Muni Lal and his wife sat down to drink readymade oversweetend coffee.

They went to Naggar after lunch. Muni Lal asked for directions and decided to go without a guide. "Why it is that the place is described as 18-20 and 28 kilometers away? he asked". Lakshmi pointed out that it depended upon where the zero, the starting point, was. In big cities, it was usually the railway station. The Naggar town was on the other side of the river, opposite to where their hotel was located. Though in some way it was the non-fashionable, area there were many hotels and houses. "What would be the situation like at the peak holiday season in summers"? they speculated.

The destination in Naggar was the art gallery commemorating life of a Russian artist, Nikolai Roerich and his well-known Indian wife, Devika Rani. The location was above the road they came by on a well-maintained passage. There was a castle on the way but it did not look conspicuous. Muni Lal and Lakshmi spent time carefully looking at the artifacts but their thoughts were somewhere else. Lakshmi said when they were away, "One has to have a real liking for this kind of life. Without modern facilities, one keeps worrying about cooking, heating, transportation." Neither of them was much of a follower of Indian country life. In another situation, Muni Lal said that there was not much importance of handmade things, even when they were a little imprecise when machine could do a better job. But making handmade goods gave more employment.

On the way down, they stopped at a hotel. It appeared to be closed. However, the manager was around sitting in the sun and he assured them that coffee was available. He made two chairs and a table brought out for coffee drinking and talking. "Nagger," he said, "was the capital of the region at one time." They were clever enough not to enquire about the period concerned. The manager said that there were remarkable old temples. Heun Tsang, a Chinese traveller came there and made appreciative comments about Naggar. As for his hotel, a group of Russians was there recently celebrating Roerich's birth anniversary.

They returned to the hotel. They were to leave the next morning just after the hotel gave them the breakfast. They talked about going to the main market once again but did not actually do so. They told each other that they liked Manali. They said half convincingly they would come again. They looked at the good aspects. Roads up to this comparatively remote area were good. There was no problem of water and electricity. They said that the people they met with were all nice. They were determined to be cheerful about seeing mountains and a swift flowing river from close by.

□

11

Muni Lal had telephoned Joshi from Manali and got a reassuring response that they were waiting to take action and nothing adverse was to report. Back in Delhi, he contacted Watanabe and a meeting was fixed at his rented apartment in Gurgaon. It turned out to be a large residential apartment complex and actually one of the numbers of them in the neighbourhood. They all looked new. Joshi was also there at the meeting. The apartment was large. 'The Japanese company was keeping its representative in good condition thought,' Muni Lal. The place was neat and clean with little decoration, besides furniture, a music system and a golf set.

Watanabe said that he was regularly reporting developments to Osaka. "The jobs for them," he said "were two-fold." The headquarter was insisting that the Indian group should overcome any chance of delay. First of all, the allotment of land was to be there. Secondly, they should achieve it without having to pay any huge bribes. Joshi and Rohatgi were engaged in finding out the composition of the committee that would meet candidates seeking plots of land. Then an effort was to be made to meet whomever it was possible to do and seek support and enlightenment. Muni Lal could meet senior people in Delhi or in Chandigarh and ensure that their case was not going to face difficulties.

He waited for comments but did not receive any.

"In any case," Watanabe said, "what exactly do we know about this bribery business?"

Joshi said that one heard different versions from different people. "One opinion is that Indian buyers are pressurised more than the foreigners because Indians many times act for speculative purposes and could, therefore, be willing to pay. They will buy at Government rate and sell it later on to other parties at market rate. The difference in price can be more than double." "But," intervened Muni Lal, "there are regulations against the sale of land acquired from the government." "Regulations say that the land is not to be sold within one year. Boundary wall has to be made. Some construction on land has to be visibly available. A claim has to be made that a production unit has been installed. Minimum requirement is not too difficult to be complied with."

Having quietened Muni Lal, Joshi continued.

"It is maintained that foreign parties will not be harassed. They are not buying speculatively. Also, foreign investment has to be visible in the country. But the third view is that there are few exceptions unless when there is some political connection."

"What is the rate of the payment expected?" asked Watanabe.

"It is not exact. There are variations." Joshi spoke in a worldly wise fashion.

"But generally people will say 2% of the price of the land". "So, it means," said Watanabe, "if we have to pay Rs. 80 crore to the government, we have to pay another Rs. 1.6 crore." Watanabe had learned to count in Indian style.

"Looks like it. Government people say that the buyers get land from them at a cheaper rates as compared to buying from farmers or other private parties. So, the officials should get a share of saving." Joshi explained in neutral tone.

"What I wonder is whether some critics are not present. Surely everybody in the department cannot be in it. I have been a government servant myself," Muni Lal said.

"Money is shared. It does not go to one pocket or a couple of them." Watanabe decided to intervene, feeling as if a disagreement was creeping in.

"We will deal with the bees when we come to the bee-hive. What we are concentrating on is getting the land and doing so with as little extra cost as possible."

"And the extra payment has to be made in cash," Joshi said.

"And not by cheque," added Muni Lal pointing out the obviousness of the matter. Muni Lal had started feeling it was his turn to say something.

"People in the various ministries in Delhi are not going to be of much help. In any case, one has to hit upon a right ministry and right officers. I am thinking that I should list out the officers from my batch who are living in Delhi or, if necessary, in Chandigarh. Then among them to sort out those with Haryana connection—whether having worked there or belonging to the region. The first type will be directly helpful."

"That will be a good idea," said Watanabe.

"That will be a good idea," added Joshi. He may differ with Muni Lal but was anxious to endorse Watanabe.

There was nothing more to discuss but, as is natural, they were reluctant to disperse. Watanabe showed them the flat. One room contained gadgets like a computer, a photocopier and a fax machine and, of course, the telephone. No bedroom was shown. The kitchen looked modern but there was not any talk of servants.

□

12

Muni Lal looked through the list of people who joined the senior government service in the same year as he. He seemed to know few of them except those in his own service. Ultimately, he managed to choose three who retired from administrative service who lived in Delhi and who had worked in Haryana.

He started by contacting Dayal Kishan. He introduced himself as a batch mate and requested for a meeting. Dayal Kishan agreed but asked at the same time what was the objective. Muni Lal was careful not to say that he needed help. He mentioned that he needed some information about Haryana State set up. He reached the destination 10 minutes in advance and moved around to while away time. Seeing him on the dot, Dayal Kishan expressed his appreciation. He said that he also was very punctual. His first district officer drilled the need of it into him. Muni Lal and Dayal Kishan could not place each other by look or by known activities in the few months they had spent together during collective training all those years ago. Muni Lal gave him his card to officialise the visit.

There was no hurry to come to the point. There were quite a few framed miniature paintings hanging on the walls. Muni Lal went over them and expressed his admiration. Were they acquired in Haryana? Dayal Kishan was ready to go over the details. Some of them were old and belonged to his father. Others he himself had purchased at various places. Muni Lal said that he was highly impressed. There were some family photos also but Muni Lal did not enquire about them.

The maid brought tea and snacks. Dayal Kishan said that his wife was away and his regular servant also left recently. He said that he asked for some days' leave, but now might not come back. The maid was new. Muni Lal said that he was deeply aware of troubling the household. They discussed the servant situation in Delhi.

Muni Lal felt politeness required him to start discussion of the Japanese company rather than force Dayal Kishan to ask why he was there.

"Do you have an employment after retirement?" Muni Lal enquired.

"No, no," said Dayal Kishan emphatically, which could also be considered to be an effort to conceal his work.

"I am appointed as an advisor to a Japanese company setting up a factory in the Haryana state. Our application for grant of land, I mean allotment, not gifting, has been accepted to the extent that we will be called for an interview by a committee."

"Has a date of the interview been fixed?"

"We have no information yet."

"Please proceed."

"We naturally want that the process should be gone through quickly. We also want that we do not have to pay any extra amount, you know. We are a serious and genuine party. The company is incurring daily expenditure. I have come to seek guidance on how to accomplish our goal. You have experience and you were in a higher service than I."

"Please do not say that. It is not important. I have known people entering service at the end of the list and finishing off at the top."

"Our two questions are together—How to succeed quickly? How to avoid unnecessary payment?"

"It is true that bureaucracy is not as clean as it used to be. But the politicians in power are also to be blamed for it. I will like to tell you of one case. When I was given my first district, there was a project needing clearances and a no-objection certificate. The party, the company who had taken up the job, came to me with a member of the legislative assembly. They said that the project was of national importance and brooked no delay. I told them that proper scrutiny would have to be gone through. Some payments were hinted at to me and I showed them the door. The MLA in any case was not from the ruling party. They could not find somebody else."

They both laughed. "This is a good one," said Muni Lal. "The company did not manage to bring somebody from the ruling party."

They continued after the pause.

"You will be knowing state officers of today. They are all junior to you. I request you to spare us some time. Please come with us to Chandigarh. You do not have to bother about transport, accommodation, etc."

"I am out of the loop now. I know the Chief Secretary of the state. I can pick up the telephone and call him. We worked in the same district one after the other. I went there earlier. But it will not work. He would say that we should go to the secretary concerned. In any case, he is a non-smoker, non drinker, vegetarian, religious type." Muni Lal took the name of joint secretary Satyapalan. Dayal Kishan said that he did not know him. Muni Lal said that if he came with them that is Watanabe included he was bound to meet people he knew.

Dayal Kishan said that in bureaucracy what was proper was to go to the top. They should reach the secretary in charge. They should not, of course, speak of not wanting to pay any bribe.

"Such things as you know are not mentioned."

"You and I are from the same fraternity. There is bound to be an occasion for us to help each other."

"Another group of people you can consider approaching is the industrialists. They have a great influence over the government officials." Muni Lal thought of asking him if he knew any but let go. Mulling the situation, he realised that Dayal Kishan could actually not do anything. The saving grace was that he was not making promises.

"I will make a move. I had a very useful discussion for which I am grateful." "I wish you success. Our industry has to grow. Foreign money and technology are welcome. Do let me know how things work out. If you think it is necessary that I should speak to the Chief Secretary, do not hesitate to come back. It is good to meet you after so many years."

□

13

The next day Muni Lal decided to take things easy and to keep away from investment matters. He and Lakshmi went to Ajmal Khan market, the big market in Karol Bagh. Making use of past experience, he entered from the road facing the Muslim and Hindu medical college and parked near one of the entrances to Ajmar Khan park.

"He was a great Hakim, a Muslim medicine man," Muni Lal said of Ajmal Khan.

"There are Hindu Hakims also," said Lakshmi. Muni Lal and Lakshmi exchanged glances confirming many years of togetherness. Crossing the road into the proper market area and leaving the small eateries and fruit shops had a system of its own. There was not much use of a traffic light. When a pressure built up, people crossed over in strength bringing vehicles to a halt, though a motor cycle or two managed to get away by less than a yard.

The market was as usual very crowded. Pavement shoppers spilled into the road. "The shops are not all that crowded," said Muni Lal.

"They are just window shoppers."

"Like us," said Lakshmi and Muni Lal gave a glance by way of acknowledgement.

The shops were predominantly of garments and textiles, of jewellery, including artificial jewellery, leather goods and beauty accessories. It was not so much a place for household food ingredients except for canned items. Narrow side lanes were packed with small shops and customers, everyone talking. Some shops advertised discounts of 50% and even more.

"These discounts are for a fixed number of days. Suppose today is the last day," said Lakshmi.

"Suppose I come tomorrow. Will they charge me 40% more for an item now on display?"

"It may not be there tomorrow."

"I can understand garments being removed and taken away into stores with change of season. But they do not have to remove shoes and things of that kind."

"Shops must be making profits even by giving 50% discount."

"Do you think they write higher prices before giving discounts?" asked Lakshmi. "This would have been easier before maximum retail price was stamped on items," suggested Muni Lal.

"It comes to my mind that these things are defective. The shops write over their announcements that the items once sold can't be returned or replaced."

"I was thinking of another matter," Muni Lal said when outside the shop which spoke of 50% discount.

"Inside the discount is going to be given on items on a few shelves only."

They stopped at a shop selling Bengali sweets. Such shops have a great name. Most eating places were selling Indian rather than western items. Inside there was a pervasive smell of sugary things. They bought their stuff and carried the packet out rather than eat there.

Lakshmi stopped outside a children goods shop. There were toys and clothing. She said, "We will have to buy infants' items." Muni Lal gave her an enquiring look. "It is quite some months away," she said.

"I did realise Anju was looking heavy," said the father.

"But it could have been the results of late dinners and no exercise."

"Or anal sex," Lakshimi said.

"That makes no difference," said Muni Lal defensively. They sat in the car, closed the windows to avoid beggars and dealt with the eatables.

"How is the Japanese project coming up?" asked the wife.

"There is no new development. However, one thought comes to my mind."

"As a replacemt for an action?" asked Lakshmi. Muni Lal ignored her.

"Suppose we do not do anything. Will we not get the land? Why not? Suppose we do not give any money to anybody, what will the officials do? Or the other way round, suppose all the applicants come to a decision that no money is to be given. The State government will have to allot land to the applicants; it cannot wait indefinitely."

"There was a Prime Minister of India" said Lakshmi.

"He claimed that the best way of population control was willpower exercised by couples anxious not to have many children." "Lakshmi was becoming quite cynical," said Muni Lal to himself.

□

14

Muni Lal's call on the second of the three candidates he has chosen was on Chowdhry Ram Singh. Dayal Kishan had in passing mentioned that Ram Singh had been chief secretary—for a short period—he had added.

Muni Lal seated himself and phoned at his number obtained from the list of members of the batch. He had waited till 10:00 a.m. He identified himself as Ram Singh picked up the phone.

"Where are you from?" he was asked.

"I studied in Delhi," said Muni Lal.

"So did I," replied Ram Singh. They checked up the names of colleges they went to and the subjects they studied.

"I phoned to ask you if I could meet you for half an hour or so and collect some information about Haryana. I can come to your house at your convenience."

Ram Singh said that they could meet at his club the next day. He and his wife were scheduled to be there as per an earlier programme. A time was fixed.

Muni Lal said to himself that this was perhaps his best chance now. He went to the destination and waited. No sign of the host. He went to some waiters and told them that he was waiting for Chowdhry Ram Singh and he should be identified to him if necessary when he arrived. An hour passed. Muni Lal had left Ram Singh's phone number at home. He began to say to himself that he would leave after this or that time but continued to stay pot.

At last the couple arrived. The wife, though she should be 60 was dressed gaudily as if for a function and looked naughty. Her being rather plump did not bother her one bit.

"I can't say I remember you," said Ram Singh.

"We were rather a close group of administrative service trainees. What did you study?"

"I studied chemistry."

"That explains it. We did not meet during student days. My subject was economics. It was the biggest group in the college and in the university."

"It still is. It still is," said Muni Lal hoping it will be a welcome statement. "Our time of training together was a short one as you know."

Muni Lal looked dignified. Ram Singh decided to give an explanation for their delay.

"We were to attend a function at the President Palace. We are coming from there. Yesterday I forgot about it when I fixed appointment with you. This morning I phoned your landline but nobody picked up. Your cell number was dead."

"My wife was to be out of the house in the morning. I have changed my mobile number but I left your mobile number at home."

"In any case," said Ram Singh, "they take away mobile phone at the reception at the Rashtrapati Bhavan. I think it is a good practice."

Muni Lal told them in clear terms the purpose of his seeking a meeting with Ram Singh.

"You are the most useful person for our purpose, We do not want delays. The paper work has to get cleared quickly and we do not want to pay out unnecessarily."

"Nobody wants to pay extra. It is natural," said the wife. Ram Singh was interested in the matter. He asked what Muni Lal liked to have from the restaurant. His modest requirement was added to by the couple.

Muni Lal gave the names of Joint Secretary Satyapalan. He said he would go to Chandigarh and meet him if Ram Singh gave him a letter to carry.

"These things are not reduced to writing. I can telephone. I do not have to know them. They have to know me. But the project clearance can cost money. Work in offices is slowing down. What will you do if you are told that an officer is not at his seat or out of town?"Ram Singh's wife made tea for the three.

"What games do you play?"she asked Muni Lal.

"I do not play any outdoor games now. I used to play badminton. It is a fast game. My wife and I play chess sometimes."

"Please teach us also" she said.

"I will be very happy to come to your house and do so. Actually the rules are simple. But the possibilities of movements are huge."

They were quiet for a while. Muni Lal realised that Ram Singh would need some payment if the job had to be successfully gone through. It was not a payment for transport to and accommodation in Chandigarh only. He thought of asking how much it would cost. The Japanese could be persuaded to pay. But will they particularly if the amount was large? Such matters got tangled into one party asking for payment in advance and the other promising to do so after the job was implemented. It appeared that the couple was anxious to leave.

"I will seek an appointment with Satyapalan. Please ring him up tomorrow just making him to see me. I will take care of the rest."

"If I have to get involved in this, which I can do successfully, I would like to meet your superiors to thrash out the terms. Ultimately, you people will be saving some money also."

Back home, Muni Lal rang up Dayal Singh in Chandigarh. He gave his name and mentioned

Delhi. After some times a reply came on the line from a lady that Dayal Singh was not available.

He telephoned Satyapalan. He told his secretary that he was coming to Chandigarh and would like to have a meeting with the JS at his convenience about the Japanese company's project. He was their advisor. The secretary spoke respectfully. "It was," he said, "lunchtime and Muni Lal had to call later." He did after two hours and was told that JS had come but now gone to a meeting. Muni Lal tried once before closing time. He was told that he got late. The personal secretary himself was not able to speak to the JS about the appointment that was sought. It would be best for him to come to Chandigarh and stay there, come to their office and take his chance. The JS was rather busy around this time of the year. Muni Lal wrote a letter to Ram Singh and posted it in the evening itself. It would reach him the day after tomorrow, he calculated. "It was very nice meeting you and your gracious wife this morning. It was a happy experience to meet somebody after a long interval with whom you were in the same university and then joined the government service the same year. Your performance at work has been absolutely creditable. I also did well in my department. Getting the Japanese project through is now a matter of *izzat* to me. We should get the land for building a factory, not pay anybody extra beyond the land cost. Now that India is attracting foreign investment—at least in some states—it is to the credit of the leaders and government officials. It is requested you may make a telephone call to the investment authorities about my coming to Chandigarh and I should be given a little time when I seek a meeting. We may not ask for a specific time for an appointment. I will ring you up the day after tomorrow and with your blessing get prepared to leave for Chandigarh." He went over the text. He amended "pay anybody" to "anybody in Chandigarh". There was no point excluding Ram Singh.

He phoned him at lunch time as promised. Postman must have arrived. Ram Singh was brusque, "I had thought of making a call to the state government but feel it would not serve a purpose. You should make the Japanese owners to meet me. They are sensible people in my experience." Muni Lal offered to visit Ram Singh's house to discuss matters in detail. Ram Singh said that it was not necessary. They had a discussion after all only two days ago.

Muni Lal felt that it was going to mean asking the Japanese to pay Ram Singh. There might even be a suspicion that Muni Lal himself was in the scheme and liable to collect a bit from Ram Singh. He had consistently talked of managing to avoid giving bribes.

In the evening, Muni Lal sat on a bench at a park not far from his house. Days were becoming shorter. Twilight coloured the clouds and tended to disappear by six in the evening. The light did not hurt the eyes as it did in summer. The park was oval in shape. Muni Lal could walk around it on the tiled pavement in three minutes. He used to sit for some minutes, watch people, trees, and birds and then take another round. An hour's outing was refreshing.

As usual there were more women than men walking round the park. It was supposed to be a good exercise for reducing weight and it was a common thought among the Hindus not very far from their minds that it improved thinking and feeling. He could not feel that he had seen cases of reduced weight. But he remembered the story once told to him by a colleague from South India. A man went to an astrologer to find out how the day would work out. The astrologer said that he was to gain money that day. Actually he lost some amount. He went back to the astrologer to complain. He was told that he was to lose much money but did not. So, he was a gainer. In the same way, the ladies, if they did not do walking, they would gain weight. He did not feel very satisfied.

He tried to lose himself in happy imagining. He was visiting European cities with his girlfriend. They were together in the class. He never managed to speak to her. Even her face was blurred to him now. But the impression that once he just was 6 inches away from her shapely bottom remained strong. He moved over smoothly to a hockey match, though he never played the game. The team was a goal behind with only three minutes left of regulation time. People switched off their radios and TV sets. One family walked out, not talking much, ran into a crowd of boys shouting and singing and dancing. When asked, they simply said, "He has done it. He first scored the equalizer and then a winning goal in extra time."He thought of going home and listening to recorded songs. His wife and he had CDs that were personal choice but not so much collective. He could listen to ghazals at home, he thought. But he felt tired. Alcohol and sex came to his mind and left him unenthusiastic.

Lights started coming in the houses surrounding the park. After a while, the park lights switched on. Muni Lal saw one of the lights was not working. What was the worst was what would happen to him if the Japanese project failed. His salary would come to an end. It was a temporary thing in any case. He decided to encounter the third and last retired senior administrative officer who served in Haryana.

□

15

Kuldip Kapoor responded to his telephone call enthusiastically. "Most welcome, most welcome," he said and they agreed to meet the next day.

It was a well appointed house. Muni Lal did not, could not know if Kapoor owned the whole place or a part of it. He was operating from a detached room downstairs. There were papers and invitation cards on the table. Muni Lal had come in after waiting 15 minutes some distance in his car. Kapoor hugged him and coffee was asked for through the chowkidar.

The work of placing each other started carefully. They realized that they studied in the same university. This was a very satisfying matter for Kapoor. Muni Lal also relaxed. They worked out that a large number of senior government servants came from their university. Muni Lal did not think it necessary to say that Chowdhry Ram Singh was also one of them. The fact that there were so many ministries and departments in existence, where the senior officials were a model, an inspiration for their children was a fact duly agreed upon. They shook hands on making their discoveries. They turned to the possible persons they knew in common. Kapoor said that he used to know Tony quite well who entered the same service as Muni Lal. As Muni Lal looked uncertain, Kapoor said, "Oh! I mean Grover. Did you not know he was known at home and to friends as Tony? His father was in police although a gentleman despite his background." This witticism produced much hilarity.

Talking about families was but a natural next step. Muni Lal volunteered that his wife was from Orissa.

"So, you really went far," said Kapoor.

"We were together in the university, though not in the same class. I am some four years older."

"And not the other way round," Kapoor added to much laughter.

"We got introduced. I had joined service by then."

"So, you were eligible."

"I phoned her once, asking if we could meet for coffee, and she agreed."

"Were there not any objections from the families?"

Muni Lal thought over the matter for a while.

"It was mid sixties. India is much more liberal now. It was a job to bring her home once to meet the family."

"The family might have asked what the relationship was."

"It had to come out that we wanted to marry. Not during her visit, I mean. The interesting thing is the caste was not too much of a problem. I think difference in caste is more of a problem if the two persons are from the same state than otherwise."

"So, congratulations all around?"

"The one great objection was that she was not very fair. How could I say that that was one of her strong points for me? Slowly my mother came out with the view that such girls are not good. I mean those who come to know boys all by themselves. My parents told me that they had not even seen each other before marriage. Family background only was important."

"Who in the family was your backer?"Kapoor wanted to know.

"Many people wanted to know details of relationship. Where were we meeting? Did we go to movies together? They thought that I was a bit of a lady killer but gave no public endorsement."

"So, you had some sleepless nights?"

"Father said that he would put up a matrimonial advertisement. Many responses would have come.

We could make a wise choice. Mother said that it was not as if they would arrange things without duly taking my consent."

"How did it work out in the end?"

Kuldip Kapoor was enormously interested. Muni Lal continued.

"Went to her house also. I was determined to say to the father that I had come to ask for his daughter's hand. But the subject never came up."

"What was he?"

"A doctor. There were many practical problems. When the two parents met, my mother's big complaint was that her parents did not seem to speak Hindi, which actually they did."

"How does your wife look back at the situation?"

"We both realized that it was a new experience for all of us. We are forgiving. After all, we managed it. But practical problems remained. What kind of a marriage was it to be? North Indian style or East Indian style?"

"So what was it?"

"Oh, North Indian. But they did later on organize a ceremony of their own. So, it was a marriage and a half. I got government accommodation and living separately by ourselves helped. But there were questions we had not even thought of. What kind of food to eat? We had to sit down to decide how much to take of one, how much of other and how much western. She is a good cook."

"Of course, of course. You are a living example of a love marriage of which we see examples in movies."

"Where heroes and heroines do not have caste names even, only first names."

Muni Lal provided a witticism this time.

"How are you keeping yourself busy after retirement?" he asked, trying to come to his objective.

"I am with a tourism company. I am behind the scenes entertaining people and working out details of programmes to be offered. You know making the hotels in Bangkok to agree to provide a free drink to guests in our group on arrival and so on. I was at one time special secretary to the chief minister. One of my jobs was to keep people happy in their dealings with the C.M. But the regime changed. A new government came and I got a slightly obscure job. For some time only. I was not hurt in any way."

They talked of their children. They were pleasantly surprised to learn that each one had one daughter only.

"Mine is married to a businessman in Ludhiana."

"We are trying to arrange a match for ours," said Kapoor.

"I also have a small temporary job. It is concerning that I am troubling you. I am working as an advisor to a Japanese company wanting to set up a production unit in Haryana. They are making some electronic components of automobiles."

"Have you been called for an interview?"

"We have received the call. The date has not been fixed yet. We want the allotment of the land to take place quickly and without having to pay any bribes."

"What kind of rate have you heard about?"

"2% of the land price."

Kapoor was quiet. Muni Lal pressed on. "Your position is most helpful. What we need is a message to be given to the Department, to take care of our case, I have the necessary names and telephone numbers with me here."

"I wish I can provide help. There was a time even three years ago when I could make a call to Chandigarh and the job was done. The change of the government changed things."

"You can please try."

"You do not have to ask me twice. We are like brothers but officials have sensitive antenna. If they hear from you, they will work out what is your strength. I am not in politics. I am against any political party. Why should I be involved? I am not electioneering for any candidates but the officials will not move if they hear from me. Time will change again, though I am aware you can't wait for that."

"There must be some suggestion you can make, some advice you can give."

"Mind you, I am not in favour of paying and receiving money. I am an honest man. But a system has come into existence. It is unfortunate. Political changes only make marginal differences."

Muni Lal said, "It is a question of what kind of a contribution I am making to the project."

When Kapoor suggested more coffee, Muni Lal thought of taking leave.

"We must meet again," said Kapoor. "The wives should also meet. Mine was a traditional marriage," he added.

□

16

Muni Lal spent a few quiet days. He arranged his books, his clothes, his shoes, polished them also. He walked in the park and listened to music. He asked Lakshmi to go out with him in the evening, to which she readily agreed.

At last, Watanabe received an intimation that he and his group should appear in Chandigarh for an interview for the state government to know in detail about their proposed production unit. He told Muni Lal and Joshi that they should reach Chandigarh three days in advance. Joshi was to organize hotel and go with Watanabe in his vehicle. Watanabe asked Muni Lal to contact Dayal Singh. "He," Watanabe said, "seemed to be the most helpful person."

Muni Lal contacted Dayal Singh during the journey itself while he was halting for a cup of tea. He was told that Dayal Singh was out of town for a week having left only the day before.

In Chandigarh, Rohatgi joined them. Muni Lal's story was soon told. There were no new efforts he could make. He mentioned the people he met and received sympathetic nods.

Of the ten or so persons, who would make the interview board, the names were generally known now. There was a finance man whom Rohatgi knew from his father, the professor's time. He and Joshi were to go to his house. Muni Lal was not involved.When they came back in the evening, they talked seriously to Watanabe. Muni Lal asked what had been accomplished but got no reply. In course of time, Watanabe said that they met a person who had taken part in such interviews before. He was good enough to say that questions would be asked if it was a joint venture, or a 100% investment, if all money was available and also questioned about the nature of items to be produced. The interview would also want to be satisfied that the Japanese were not polluting environment in the production operations.

A day before they had another visit to the bar where Muni Lal took one more drink than his usual limit.

In the morning, Muni Lal offered to give Rohatgi a lift but the latter went with the others saying that something might come up for discussion.

It was in the main hall of the building that they knew well by now that they went. It was large but enough people were there already to create the feeling that ultimately the chairs would fall short in number. Watanabe and Muni Lal sat down adjacently, not having anything to say to each other. Joshi and Rohatgi were busy moving about together, going upstairs also but showing that they were not finding a person they wanted to meet.

It was the beginning of winter. In North India, there was a saying that winter stayed from Diwali to Holi but ceiling fans were still working. People were dressed in a variety of costumes. There were those in suits and neckties but also a good number in the usual shirts and trousers. More conservative long shirt and dhoti were not absent. Only one gentleman sported the politician's dress of kurta - pajama - waist coat and Gandhi cap. And then there were also seen some closed collar coats.

Muni Lal went to the notice board to see if there was an order in which people were to be called. He saw two lists and found their company's name in one of them. There was another Japanese company listed. Looking around, he found two other Japanese sitting together conferring. There were few women. Joshi and Rohatgi came and said that they were in the first list of those to be interviewed before lunch. They showed that they had managed the listing. The second list people were to be met only in the afternoon.

Rumour started that interview had already begun in the closed room. But as no candidates seemed to be coming and going, the rumour subsided.

Most people were serious and carried various papers. Watanabe also did. However there was one Indian who was laughing and smiling nearly all the time. He had three foreigners, looking European, with him. Muni Lal got the impression that he was an important and influential agent leading clients through such interviews. This could not be the first time. He gave the impression, or was trying to do so, that getting the job done was nothing more than a laugh for him or a game he could play even with his left hand as the saying went.

People started going in to meet the interview board. They did not stay in long, some five or six minutes. They came back through the same door they went in. The officials had obviously gone in through another special entrance. Some people tried to get in when the earlier group came out. They were stopped by the gate-keeper and their name checked whether their turn had actually come. The foreign party with the cheerful Indian agent now came out, their turn over. The Indian looked satisfied as before saying as if this was it and just a formality with me being there.

The four-member Osaka party had their turn now. Actually, they had already stationed themselves near the entrance. It was a biggish room with a number of chairs for the clients. Watanabe and Muni Lal sat in one row and Joshi and Rohatgi behind them. There were eight or nine officials.

Three of them were sitting in one row, facing the candidates. There were others on the two sides taking notes, providing information. No names were mentioned. But Muni Lal thought that the man in the middle must be Satyapalan both because of his position and his South Indian look. North Indians are tea-coloured and South Indians are coffee coloured, foreigners are usually told.

The man in the middle turned to one on his side to check up as if they had the right party before them.

The first two questions were on the expected lines—was it going to be a Joint Venture or a completely foreign owned investment? And did the Japanese party have the resources for purchasing land and the subsequent expenditure? Watanabe answered them but the two sitting behind him kept whispering the obvious answers.

The party was to make specialized items for the automobile industry. Did it have buyers in India or was the product meant for export? The answer was given that there were Indian buyers. Indian automobile industry was expanding and the Haryana state was ideally situated for production. In course of time, it might be possible to export some portion. The man in the middle asked one on the side to ask any questions. He asked aggressively if they were prepared to overcome pollution. Watanabe said that theirs would not be a polluting industry. In any case, they would collect all the necessary certificates before commencing production.

"What would be the cost?" asked one official.

"The estimate of cost of land, construction and machinery has been prepared by us," Watanabe said. He held out three or four copies of typed paper. Muni Lal sitting next to him took them to the high officials without looking at anybody. Watanabe said that the cost of employment would need to be looked at later on.

"How many do you intend to employ?"

"About one hundred at its peak, both white colour and blue colour."

"And 98% will be Indian," Rhotagi added excitedly.

"You can have me too," said one of the senior officers.

The man in the middle smiled as if to say that he was not against a sense of humour. Others followed suit.

"What can you tell us about your product?"asked the top man.

Joshi rushed to the dais with a metallic component about half a kg in weight. Watanabe brought it from Delhi but Muni Lal had not seen it.

One senior officer touched it with curiosity. Watanabe could have explained its working but the chief gave the nod and the interview was over.

Joshi and Rohatgi said that it went off well, they should be fully satisfied. Watanabe said that he appreciated their effort to collect necessary information.

Muni Lal said that he would now go back to Delhi. He said that he had vacated the hotel room in the morning.

Only half an hour later he got a call on his mobile from Watanabe. "Thank you very much for your work. There will be no need to contact Dayal Singh anymore."He pronounced the name as Dayaru.

"If I do it, that will be only to thank him," Muni Lal answered. He was satisfied with his repartee. Were Joshi and Rohatgi asking Watanabe that Muni Lal should not interfere? He felt depressed.

He stopped his car and telephoned Lakshmi. "It is all right as far as it goes."

"It is very nice to hear that. They will be very happy at the amount of hard work you put in." Lakshmi gave her view.

"What I wanted to say was that nothing went wrong today. There is a lot of work yet to be done."

Lakshmi could feel from his voice that he was not satisfied.

"What is your programme?"

"I am on my way home."

"Will you like me to do some preparation?"

"It is not like Shri Rama returning to his Kingdom after 14 years of exile."

But Muni Lal thought that he was being nasty to Lakshmi who was only trying to be friendly. "Let us go out somewhere," he added.

"You will be tired."

"Oh I will be all right after half an hour's rest."

They decided to go to a movie. It was the fourth in the series depicting ship journey from Chennai to Singapore. These movies were an obvious result of economic growth in India as otherwise such voyages were not common or desirable.

This one was advertised as suspenseful and with crime detection. In the beginning, various personages were entering the ship and moving about in various areas. Some of these passengers were known actors, whose appearance was greeted by spectators and their names loudly pronounced.

A few hours after the ship started there was entertainment for the whole group in the hall of the ship. Children were absent. A well known actress, who was to be called an actor as a matter of courtesy gave, a vigorous dance recital while singing at the same time. She was wearing skin tights and was meant to be provocative and half dressed. The song by itself was a popular item number in the country by now.

There were thefts reported on the ship, mostly of the jewellery. By various hints and suggestions, the dancer who is the heroine and always to be so, was herself a suspect.

The audience knew in the heart of hearts that the heroine was innocent. To make her criminal was to take too much of a chance, a risk with people's expectations. The hero is actually a detective. He and the heroine confessed their love to each other wearing swimming costumes. The hero undergoes mental torture having to make up his mind between love and duty. He sings a mournful song.

The crime situation becomes worse. At last, the hero decides to take action by confronting the heroine. She is actually a detective herself. They hit upon some clues separately. The two criminals, one of them foreign-looking and speaking strained Hindi are chased. There is a good deal of running up and down, same members of the journey becoming caught in cross fire as shooting begins. The heroine starts singing her words, cautioning the hero of the danger when it appears and also hinting where to look for. The end comes with a good deal of noise, the criminals trying to run away in a motorboat in which the loot is also tightly secured but are caught. The captain of the ship is very satisfied and happy. He finds a priest and a proper marriage ceremony is arranged with Singapore in sight.

They had difficulty taking their car out of the parking. Everybody was trying to reach the exit at the same time. There were also drivers coming in wrongly through the exit. There was a lot of honking. But these things get sorted out eventually. "She was looking good," said Lakshmi.

"Despite her age," said Muni Lal.

Lakshmi gave him a conspiratorial look.

Muni Lal was too intelligent to praise the heroine to his wife.

□

17

The days passed slowly. Winter was approaching with sun setting by 6 p.m. and not being very bright in the day also. One evening after dinner, Muni Lal suggested to his wife that they should have coffee. She suggested tea as otherwise they might have difficulty in sleeping. Muni Lal became irritated, feeling that his wife tended to be contradictory.

One evening Muni Lal was surprised by the visit of Rohatgi. He said that he had come from Chandigarh at his own initiative and was going to stay with Joshi. If necessary, they could all go together to meet Watanabe. They enquired about each other's family. Lakshmi came and Rohatgi was suitably deferential. Lakshmi organized drinking of whisky for them. Gradually, they came to the subject of the Japanese project.

"How soon should we be knowing the decision about the grant of land?" asked Muni Lal.

"It should not take too much longer. Usually, the majority of those who are called for interview are accommodated, not rejected. After all they are a source of payment to the officials and I should think leaders." Rohatgi made it sound like a humorous situation but he became duly serious.

"Naturally not much payment can be had till now."

"Suppose the state government sends us a letter that it is willing to allot us land, will it not solve the problem? Why should we give any bribes after that?"

"We have not got the letter of allotment. The time of payment is now so that the letter comes trouble-free."

"Suppose we do not get the letter. Can we not ask for an explanation?"

"Who you will ask? In any case, the government is not obliged to give an explanation. If anybody applies for the visa to an embassy but does not get it, he cannot ask for an explanation."

"What should a party seeking allotment of land do next?"

"It will have to apply again."

"Do you mean that we keep waiting now and ultimately nothing positive may happen?"

"I will tell you what happened a couple of days ago. I got a call from a person saying that he wanted to speak to me about the Japanese project. I asked him about his name and he would not disclose it. He said that if we gave him Rs. 2.0 crore, he will hand over to us the letter of land allotment. I said that I wanted to meet him and discuss details before I could approach our people. We had to give up."

"I do not think this kind of thing could work. It is a lot of money to carry. Suppose we are waylaid by a gang belonging to this man and robbed on the way to the designated place, it would be difficult to complain to the police even. I cannot think him succeeding with any client."

Muni Lal refreshed their drinks.

"You may be knowing these things. So, I will like to be enlightened. Suppose we make up our mind to pay. What is the next step for us to take?"Rohatgi said with conviction, "We have to approach private secretary to the joint secretary Satyapalan. We have to say that we are in a hurry to get things over. There is a good deal of daily expenditure. After that, there will be negotiation about the amount. But first of all he will have a clearance from the JS."

"There are all kinds of practical matters that come to my mind. The Japanese will have to bring the money from their country and get it converted."

"No problem. They have to bring bigger amount to pay for the land."

"But that can be done bank to bank. Suppose we get the money in a bag or a number of bags. Where do we take it?" asked Muni Lal.

"The details will be agreed upon with the PS. Four of us, Watanabe, yourself, Joshi and myself can be in one car with money. The other party, most likely containing PS and a JS relative, may be even a lady, will lead in another car."

"Where will we go? Can it be the JS house?"

"It can be. It can be a relative's house. The money will be received and the official letter delivered."

"It will take a lot of time to count the money."

"Not so if the money is in high value notes and neatly bundled. And an attempt to cheat by the client should not work. The government always has many irons in the fire. Some counting will, of course, be done. The whole thing may last ten minutes, at most fifteen. The two sides will shake hands and the transaction will be over."

"The money will need to be parcelled out."

"Theys are used to it."

"I find it hard to believe this."

"You will not be the only party going through the arrangement and there will be parties who have done this process more than once."

Muni Lal seemed to have no questions left to ask. Rohatgi said, "We have to meet Watanabe. There is not too much time. We should tell him that negotiation may be started to decide upon the amount to be passed out. The three of us, yourself, Joshi and I should speak in one voice. We have to be practical and take the best line available. It was my duty, I felt, to come and discuss the matter with you."

"But I was involved to see that the job was done quickly and with the least expenditure possible."

"We know that. Your performance will be written in golden letters as my father would have said about the performance of Maharana Pratap. My father was a professor. I can hope that, through your efforts, the percentage to be paid can come down. We have to see Watanabe. I can ask Joshi to approach him and fix a meeting. I take it that you agreed to the option available to us."

"I have to think."

"This is a business like any other business. If we are successful with the department, we can work for other clients in future. There is a saying that a hint is enough to a wise man. You are my father's age. I do not have to say more."

Rohatgi left thanking the host for the drink. Lakshmi came and asked Muni Lal not to drink more. He poured himself a drink and said it was the last. Lakshmi said that there was a telephone call when there was a visitor present and she did not want to disturb Muni Lal. The call was from Kuldip Kapoor who alongwith his wife was inviting them to dinner the next day. Lakshmi had promised to give a reply quickly after consulting the husband. Muni Lal said that dinners took too long but they could respond by offering to come for tea. Kapoor protested that he was sorely disappointed by the refusal for dinner but the meeting for tea the next day was fixed.

□

18

Muni Lal had been to Kuldip Kapoor's house before. They met like old friends. His wife Kamlesh, a bulky lady wearing a small blouse, hugged Lakshmi and said she would consider her as her sister. Kapoor said, "We are disappointed you could not stay for dinner. We would have a longer period for talking and could have a drink of two".

His wife said, "I am not addicted to drinking but I can also have a glass in company."

"It is the same with me," said Lakshmi. Kamlesh squeezed her hand with affection. "I like Bengali people."

"I am from Orissa," said Lakshmi quietly. Kuldip heard her and remarked, "What my wife has said often enough is that she very much likes people from East India and particularly from Orissa and West Bengal."

They exchanged information about the various places they had seen in their postings. Then Kuldip thought it proper to enquire from Muni Lal how the

Japanese project of setting up a production unit in Haryana was progressing.

"It will come through; I see no objection as such. There will be some money involved, it seems."

"There is no escape. But one has to hope the charge is not as severe as in some cases."

They discussed again the interesting places they had visited in their lives. Luckily enough, pretty soon they lighted upon Manali. Both couple had been there. Kamlesh said that it was memorable the road goes along the river Beas for a long distance.

The maid brought tea things. There was a judicious mixture of sweets and savories. Kamlesh insisted that they should eat more than they were doing.

"I will compensate by drinking two cups of tea," said Muni Lal. This was received as a good humorous remark.

There was a good-sized statue of Ganesha in ivory. Lakshmi contemplated it and thought elephant head on top of the Ganesha must be tough on the God's shoulders and legs for carrying.

She decided to turn the idea out of her mind as there were people who spoke to her thoughtlessly of the gods and goddesses most prominent in Orissa. This annoyed her. She now concentrated on what Kuldip was saying.

"We were to meet you in any case. But the last time when we met, Muni Lal told me that your daughter was married in Ludhiana and that prompted us. You see, we have been in touch with a family in Ludhiana. They have a very eligible son."

Kamlesh took up the story. "We have some background knowledge of the family and the son. But we thought that your son-in-law could get us some more authentic information. It is not like old times any more. There can be cheating. People are employing secret agents to get information."

Kuldip said, "Ludhiana is a big city, perhaps the biggest in Punjab. But people can tend to hear from one another."

"What we will like you to do," said Kamlesh now quite business-like, "is to ask him if he knows anything."

"What is his auspicious name please?" asked Lakshmi.

"We will like you to telephone your son-in-law now," said Kuldip.

This was rather impromptu. Lakshmi said, "If only you had spoken to us a few days earlier. Our daughter Anju and her husband Suresh were with us on a visit."

Kuldip was ready to give the name of the family and the first name of the son. But he insisted that his own name, etc. were not to be conveyed to the son-in-law, so that he would not know from whom the enquiry was being made. Kamlesh said that it was her request that they should be referred to as a family from Kolkata if necessary. Lakshmi felt that the Kapoors were taking a calculated risk as nothing could prevent her and Muni Lal to give details about the Kapoors subsequently. Their daughter and son-in-law were even bound to ask out of curiosity.

"If Suresh does not know them, we can ask him to make discreet enquiry. After all, they are both in business as you have said."

Muni Lal dialled Suresh on Kapoor's telephone. Everybody waited silently. Anju picked up. There were excited questions and answers about welfare and then the phone was handed over to her husband, Suresh.

Suresh had many reports to give about his activities. The Kapoors waited patiently. Then Muni Lal took the initiative and said, "I phoned to talk to you about my friend and his family who have come from Kolkata. They are planning to marry their daughter to a person in Ludhiana. I will give you the name and information about the family. We want to know if you know them." Kapoor asked by gesture to be given the phone. After getting it, he said, "Son, we are friends of your parents. Ludhiana is a big city but you are both businessmen and you may be knowing him. His name is Vinay Sehgal."

"He is one of my best friends," was the reply. Kapoor's happiness was obvious from his face.

"What can you tell us, please?"

"He is doing well, he is doing well. He is only a couple of years younger than I. They have a house of their own to the best of my knowledge." Suresh spoke in generalities but positively. He added, "Do let me know if anything else you would like to get information about."

Kapoor thanked him. The telephone was moved to all the four but the discussion was over.

Kapoor said, "Now we will invite the Sehgals to come here and see our daughter. We would have liked you very much to meet her but she is away to a friend's birthday party."

Mrs. Kapoor said, "It would be very fortunate if the two daughters live together in Ludhiana. They will be close to each other, help each other like sisters."

Muni Lal said that they should make a move. The Kapoors insisted that they should stay longer. When they were to leave, there was much insistence on both sides to meet regularly.

□

19

The meeting with Watanabe was the very next morning at his house. Joshi and Rohatgi were already there when Muni Lal arrived. The two greeted him deferentially. Watanabe had employed a help and he offered tea Indian style. The Japanese style they were told would be tea, the so-called green tea, without milk and sugar.

Watanabe thanked them for coming.

"I have known you for a few months now. A good deal of work has been organized by now. We are waiting for the land allotment letter. I feel our case is good. The state government is likely to be considerate to a Japanese party. We have investment in some other countries already. Main question for us seems to be—Do we make a payment to get the letter? As Rohatgi-san lives in Chandigarh, I will ask him first. Is there any news if these letters are already being issued to some parties?" Rohatgi spoke carefully.

"There is no such news. The usual answer from the department is that the papers are circulated to the various officers for their comments, their signatures, and it can take some time."

"Why are copies not made and papers circulated to the different people simultaneously?"Watanabe mused.

"It is not done that way," said Muni Lal, who in his capacity as a retired government servant, was expected to respond.

"If there are comments, they will need to be reconciled. The file goes to the seniormost people at the end and their decision is the final." After a while, Muni Lal said, "I suggest all of us go to Chandigarh. We know various people who are connected to the important people in various ways. We go and ask them about the situation."

"The problem will be," said Joshi, "do we carry the money after converting it. It may not be easy to do it there. As for the current situation, we can check up on telephone also from here."

"Will you please contact somebody in Chandigarh?" Watanabe asked nobody in particular.

"Let me give it a try," said Muni Lal. He went to the telephone and wanted to speak to the Joint Secretary Satyapalan's office but realized that he had not brought the telephone number. However, Joshi supplied it. Muni Lal got through in the second attempt.

"My name is Muni Lal, a senior retired government officer. I am working as a special advisor to the Japanese company Shin Kansai seeking to put up a plant in Haryana. I was present at the recent interview for allotments and am a close friend of Dayal Singh whom you would be knowing. At the moment , what I want to know is when we can expect the letter of allotment of land to be issued to us."

The secretary replied respectfully.

"Sir, the file is under circulation. We can expect it to return by the end of the week. Then the letters will be duly issued."

Muni Lal told them about the response.

"This was to be expected," said Rohatgi.

"In my view," said Joshi, "we should think of making payment. It has become customary. If we go to stay in Chandigarh, it would add to expenditure. We do not know for how many days three of us will have to be in a hotel. If we do not get allotment letter, we will have to apply again after how many months we do not know at the moment and go through the process again and face uncertainty." Rohatgi said, "Even if we manage to complain to a high authority, the department can come back with the response "Look, we cleared 90% of the cases. Nobody is allowed to look into the papers as to why particular cases were rejected."

Muni Lal said, "I suggest a trip to Chandigarh. If money is needed, Mr. Wantanabe can come for a day or two to Delhi and make the necessary arrangement. It can also be checked up in the meantime if the bank there can handle it and rupees do not have to be carried to Chandigarh physically."

Watanabe gave his verdict.

"We should go again to Chandigarh. There we can work out as best as possible how many days' stay is needed."

It was decided to go after 48 hours. Muni Lal sought an appointment with Kapoor the same evening.

□

20

Muni Lal did not even tell his wife where he was going in the evening. He was well received by the Kapoor family. Kamlesh wore a Punjabi dress, obviously having belted her stomach under her shirt. The daughter, Amrita, was in western dress. She was about average in height and had features similar to her mother's as also her fair complexion. But there were tendencies to put on weight unless she followed a good health regimen. Muni Lal felt troubled that at 30, she would be middle-aged and talk of servants and prices.

"I am so glad you have come. I was thinking of calling you even today. I contacted the family in Ludhiana and they have agreed to come soon to see the girl," Kuldip explained.

Muni Lal saw that Amrita took in the conversation composedly.

"I will request you to come on that occasion, both of you I mean," said Kuldip.

"I will be very happy to come. My wife too, no doubt, unless I have to be in Chandigarh."

The servant brought scotch and soda. Kuldip got busy in making drinks. Before starting to make the fourth glass he asked the daughter, "How about you?"

"Just a few drops." Muni Lal saw that she really meant a small drink.

"Are you studying?"he asked her.

"She has finished. She is a post-graduate," her mother replied.

They clicked glasses.

"I have noticed that government servant families marry into businesses and business-men look for a match in a civil or military service," Muni Lal observed.

"The two sides wish to get together. One will assert position and the other money," his friend replied.

Kamlesh got into Muni Lal's intent quickly enough.

"Vinay Sehgal is also a post-graduate. He has studied law."

"Please tell us the date and time of the meeting as early as possible."

"I also came," Muni Lal added after the pause, "to talk to you about the project of starting a factory in Haryana by a Japanese company."

"What is the latest position? I had thought you obtained the land already," said Kapoor.

His wife and daughter left them to discuss these matters by themselves.

"We are at a critical juncture. Land allotment is to be made to various parties soon. It is our impression that some payment will have to be made – may be Rs, 1.6 crore – to get allotment."

"I think you should pay. Foreign parties as well as Indian parties keep a margin for such payment in their calculations."

"I had thought you would help. You have served in the state for many years with such distinction."

"You and I discussed this matter before. I do not have an influence now. My effort may be counterproductive."

"There will surely be many officers working today who were your subordinates. You could ask for help. You have such a friendly personality. Surely they will be having a regard for you."

"There is a saying that everybody knows somebody in police but that does not mean important matters can be settled just like that."

"You will have to think out a way." Muni Lal's attitude looked near to threatening.

Kapoor filled their glasses without saying anything. After taking a sip, he said, "I can understand how you are feeling. One feels like a failure but the money to be paid is not yours. You have made attempt to help. What more can one do?"

"There is a saying that clapping is done with both hands only. I am in a position to convey good reports about you, about your family. You know what marriage negotiations can be like. A match gets broken if there is a view that the girl's height is 5 feet 2 inches and not 5 feet 3 inches. People will not like to hear of smoking or drinking even when Punjab and Kerala have the highest consumption of alcohol."

"The state politics is in a mess. Not only the opposition is opposing, as it should, but there is also a revolt going on within the ruling party. The ruling party is trying to induct an opposition member of the legislative assembly in the cabinet. It is the Chief Minister's counterattack. This MLA used to be the minister in the previous government and I know him well."

"Please speak to him," Muni Lal said in a pleading, not aggressive, tone.

"It is not that easy. He has not become a minister yet. Then he has to see what he can do."

"He can speak to the CM to get our case cleared."

"He may promise me to do so, but will he be able to do so? There is the time factor."

"Please do telephone him and ask for a meeting tomorrow. We have to try."

Kapoor telephoned Chandigarh and apparently the MLA picked up the phone himself. Kapoor recognized his voice and said, "Sir, it is Kuldip Kapoor from Delhi. I want to be among the first to congratulate you on the invitation to you to join the government. Your skill, your steady hand is needed today in the government."

Kapoor said yes sir twice to what he heard at the other end.

"Sir, I will come to Chandigarh tomorrow. I want to have a meeting with you for fifteen minutes only. Please do not say 'no'. Anytime after lunch at your convenience will be most welcome."

Kapoor said thank you twice and put down the phone.

"It is four p.m. tomorrow." He looked important.

"I will drive. If we leave at 9:00 a.m. we will be there at the hotel by lunch time. We will have a drink or two in the evening. All charges will be taken care of by the Japanese party."

"Have a drink," said Kapoor.

"I will surely do it on the condition that my sister, your wife, joins us. After all, we have to inform her about the programme also."

Kamlesh was summoned and joined them with a small drink.

"We are going to Chandigarh tomorrow," said Muni Lal.

"With wives or without?" Kamlesh asked herself seriously.

"Without, I am afraid. It will most likely be for one day only."

"Drive carefully."

"I will certainly do that. In any case, I will go home in a cab now, leaving my car at your enclosure. No drink and drive today. I will come at 9:00 in the morning."

He telephoned Watanabe and told him that he was leaving for Chandigarh next morning for a meeting with a very important person, an important politician. Muni Lal would meet him in Chandigarh the next day and afterwards he would brief Watanabe.

On the way home, he realized that the daughter, Amrita was the name he tried hard to remember, had hardly spoken a word beyond greeting him, but in the morning, she was a little more forthcoming and insisted that Muni Lal should have a cup of coffee before going with her father. His protestation that he had breakfast before leaving home was of no avail.

In Chandigarh, they reached Girdhari Lal Maheshwari's house five minutes before 4:00 p.m. They were made to wait for 15 minutes. It was a simple unpretentious waiting room with a calendar on the wall and a couple of newspapers on the table. There were other people also waiting and speaking quietly.

When called, Kapoor went in alone promising to Muni Lal to get permission for him for attending the meeting soon. Truly enough he was called in after a few minutes. Muni Lal realized that Maheshwari was rather young. He should be forty, Muni Lal calculated. Muni Lal was introduced as the chief advisor of a Japanese company about to make a big investment in the state.

"I will like to go to Japan," said Maheshwari.

"That country has made great progress, great progress. People are talented and disciplined."

"Your going will be very nice," said Muni Lal.

Kapoor took up the matter.

"The Japanese company will be only too glad if you visit. Only consideration simply is availability of time. The company will take care of internal travel, sightseeing and meetings."

"The Japanese company," Kapoor changed the subject admirably, "is interested in making a huge investment in Haryana. There was an interview held by a group of senior officers of a number of companies, Indian and foreign, wanting to make investment. My friend Muni Lal was also present at the interview. It went off well for the Japanese company. Now is the time to hand over documents concerning allotment of land. There is a fear that our company may be called upon to make a payment."

"Has anybody asked you people for money?"Maheshwari asked Muni Lal.

"No sir. But the general impression is that most of the parties will have to go with a contribution or the letter would be withheld."

Kapoor said, "Sir, with your known commitment to clean and transparent administration, we have come to seek your help."

Maheshwari did not say anything. He looked at his watch.

"Have you been told of your portfolio?" Kapoor asked.

"Not yet. My interest is serving the people of the state, nothing more, and nothing else. I will be meeting the CM, may be even tomorrow. My presence will have a calming effect on the party. CM is not to be blamed. Now he will have better equation at the party headquarters after having managed to pick me up from the opposition."

"Please mention the Japanese company's case at the meeting with the CM tomorrow."

"There will be a lot of things to discuss. I am deadly serious against corruption."

"I am fully aware of your reputation. I have seen you in action. I have worked with you. Please put this case even as the last in your list of items for tomorrow. When you are about to leave at the meeting, just say, 'here is a Japanese company about to invest a large amount of money. Please see that their case goes through without unnecessary delays and hurdles. They are waiting for their letter of allotment of the land.' Nothing more needs to be said. He will understand."

After a gesture from Kapoor, Muni Lal handed over a piece of paper, giving details of name and address, acreage needed, cost of land, date of interview, etc.

The two of them took leave respectfully. Kapoor said, "You can see that I am capable of meeting important people within 24 hours of effort."

"How do you assess the outcome of the meeting?"

"Very good, very good. He does not make big promises but he gets things done. He has to meet the CM now."

"One thing comes to my mind," said Muni Lal seriously.

"There is an anti-defection law. If a person is elected on ticket of one party and then wants to join another, he has to resign and seek election again."

"You are finding problems for solutions. He can resign and become a private person. The same time he is picked up, made a minister and he takes oath of office. The only condition will be that he gets elected again within six months," Kapoor was reassuring.

"Well, it is not our problem."

They relaxed in the evening in the bar. The next day they met Watanabe and others at the

Chandigarh hotel. Muni Lal introduced Kapoor as a great new find. They reported their meeting with Maheshwari with panache. Among the important things mentioned was their being able to meet him so quickly.

Watanabe was grateful.

"We will stay tonight in Chandigarh but will return tomorrow. The land distribution will not take place for a week."

"How have you known?" the two former government servants asked together.

"One of the secretaries has gone abroad. He has to visit two countries. His clearance on the file is necessary."

Muni Lal and Kapoor left after lunch.

□

21

The visit of the Sehgals to the Kapoor house took place three days later. Muni Lal and Lakshmi were requested very strongly to come half an hour earlier than the Sehgals, which they did. The sitting room was cleaned up and air freshner used and furniture set carefully. There were fresh flowers. Kamlesh was wearing rather a conventional Punjabi dress but a fair amount of jewellery. Amrita was in a sari. She was sporting pearls belonging to the mother. The daughter was informed that as soon as the guests were sighted, she was to move out of the room and come only when summoned. Lakshmi saw that there were flowers in two vases in opposite portions of the room. Everybody looked a little nervous. Kapoor lit up a cigarette.

"No more after this one," his wife told him.

The Sehgals came half an hour later of the appointed time of 5: p.m. They did not apologize but said that they had difficulty in locating the house.

Vinay Sehgal appeared to be wearing a new suit. Muni Lal started calculation if the young man would be aggressive or need to be encouraged. Gradually he concluded that he was a mild person. His mother was a pinched person. The father was somewhat unexpectedly wearing a sherwani and churidars. The hosts were profusely welcoming. Muni Lal felt that, they, the two families, had never met before. Of course as per custom, photographs had been exchanged. After the subject of the weather was quickly gone over, Kapoor decided to praise Ludhiana as a great industrial centre and a symbol of Punjabi vitality and capacity for hard work. He had heard, he mentioned, that there were more Mercedes cars in Ludhiana than even in Delhi. The Delhi group was trying to see how to bring in Muni Lal and Lakshmi into discussion. Only rather fulsome introduction had been made.

The maid started bringing in tea things. Even she was groomed for the occasion and was wearing good clothes. The Kapoors had decided upon comparatively costly eatables but not gone for too much variety. The tea set was the one taken out only occasionally. The Kapoors thought that Amrita's presence could no longer be delayed. Kamlesh went in and brought her. She greeted the guests demurely and settled down. She helped her mother in making tea and handed over the cup to Vinay. It was obviously a meeting of families and only the very obvious defects or limitations of the young persons could be observed and considered.

"I also have a connection with Ludhiana. My daughter is married there. Her husband is in business. You may be knowing Suresh Vohra." Muni Lal said to Vinay.

"We have met," Vinay replied tersely. The subject was dropped.

"I had a friend who was a senior officer in accounts, Ram Lal Batra was the name. Do you know him?" asked Sehgal senior to Muni Lal.

Muni Lal thought over it. He felt truthfulness the best policy and said 'no'. Mrs. Sehgal asked Kamlesh if the house was their own or rented. Kamlesh replied, "We own it with God's blessing. The family had worked hard. They have taken care of me. Whether it is gold or garments, no dearth. When I was young, my husband said to me why I have not asked for anything for more than a month. And luckily, we have only one daughter. Everything goes to her after us."

"We pray to God that you people may live very long. You are young in any case," Mrs. Sehgal said.

Muni Lal thought that they were getting very serious and said, "We are now in Delhi and Hindi speakers. All the same we use so many English words. I do not know of Hindi equivalent for glass for example. There is a story that a man at Patna railway station asked a riksha to take him to Sachivalaya. The riksha puller did not know the way.

When the man said that he wanted to go to the Secretariat, he was taken there and the rikshaman complained that he should have been told the Hindi word 'secretariat' not a foreign word 'Sachivalay'."

This story relieved some tension. Amrita chipped in, "In college also we had a similar story. A taxi driver was familiar with the word 'University' and thought it was Hindi rather than with the word 'Vishawavidhalaya'." The Sehgals appreciated the young lady's story. Vinay also smiled and said, "There were many stories during my law student days also."

"Please do tell us," said Kamlesh.

"I am no longer a student. But I can tell you what my father said. He said that if I failed in business I would always have law to turn to."

"Oh you will not fail in business. You will make progress without stoppage," said Kuldip.

The Sehgals said that it was time to go. The Kapoors said that they should stay more and eat more.

Vinay's father said, "Now that we have met, we should continue our contact."

Kuldip asked their address in Delhi and said that they would visit them the next day. This was readily accepted. The marriage was as good as decided. If the Sehgals did not want the relation, they would have said that the next day they were going to be very busy. Muni Lal and Lakshmi stayed on for some time and were very warmly thanked. They had eaten many sweets and so decided not to drink.

Kamlesh said to Lakshmi, "Your contribution was very useful."

All that Lakshmi had said to Mrs. Sehgal was that she also could manage Punjabi. This capacity had rather confused the old lady, Mrs. Sehgal, in whose circle only Punjabi was spoken.

□

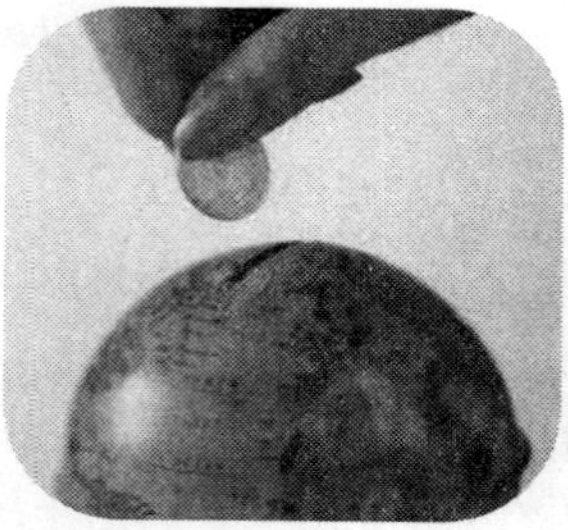

22

The trip to Chandigarh by Watanabe, Muni Lal and Joshi took place three days later. Rohatgi had learned that the letters of land allotment had started being issued and he had informed Watanabe through Joshi. At the Chandigarh hotel, they were joined by Rohatgi.

The four of them decided to go to the department office after lunch. They went in the same car, Watanabe's. There was not much to talk about during the journey.

At the office, they went straight to the person who had received their application for allotment a few months ago. To the question whether now allotments were taking place, he gave a guarded affirmative answer. They naturally asked if their company was in the list. He only said that they would have to wait. Could he not look at the list and say 'Yes' or 'No'. He said he did not have the list. Joshi and Rohatgi took him respectfully to a side and talked earnestly but they came back to say that even if the name were there in the list, the letter would not be handed over there and then. It would be sent as a registered letter to the official address in India of the company. Watanabe telephoned his house help. He had a mobile. The house help was asked to go to the house and wait outside for the postman to arrive. He should wait till 6 p.m. and come back next morning at 10 o'clock. The man grumbled that he would have to go out and eat his lunch. He was told through Joshi who promised to be persuasive that it was a matter of one day or so and Watanabe was returning himself by 6:00 p.m. that day or the next day. And others were remaining behind and promised to keep working to find out the necessary details. They did not think of going to anybody to seek help to get information. It was too late by now. It was a matter of destiny now.

Watanabe left the next morning after breakfast and three of them went to the department later in the day in Muni Lal's car, but got no new information.

The day passed slowly for the three in Chandigarh. In the evening, they thought of ringing up Watanabe. Muni Lal was chosen to do the honour. The conversation was short. There was no information to convey by either side.

The next day Rohatgi joined the other two after breakfast. They discussed news of a cricket match being played in Chennai. They separated out and then assembled at noon to go out for lunch. Just after lunch ended and they were returning to the car, Muni Lal's mobile rang. It was Watanabe's voice at the other end. The letter had arrived. The news was positive. The department had accepted the application for allotting of the land. There were some conditions. There was a last date mentioned by which the cost of land was to be paid to the state government. There were some matters concerning the actual allotment, the choice of site, etc. and it was affirmed that the authority's decision would be final. Watanabe said that he was driving back to Chandigarh.

He reached there before dinner time. They assembled in his hotel room. The bar would be too noisy. Watanabe was carrying some supply of drink. The hotel could do the rest to help. Watanabe thanked the three and said that without their help, the company could not have achieved success. Four of them considered seriously if there was any question of payment now and concluded that there was none. Muni Lal said that they did not know how exactly they had been successful, had avoided payment of some Rs. 1.6 crore. Therefore, it was not possible to say who was to be thanked. Joshi, who liked to be on the right side, said that in his view, Muni Lal's efforts indeed bore fruit. Rohatgi said that he had already spoken to three other persons in Chandigarh, who helped clients seeking land from the government. They had all paid. One of the three was particularly happy that his side had to give only 1.25% of the price of land. The meeting lasted quite a while. Watanabe had informed the headquarters in Osaka from Delhi. He said that he could sing to the three but only if he had proper background music.

He said that they should give a cocktail party in two or three days.

The letters of invitation were typed in bold letters and duplicated. The group wanted to give an advance notice of four days or so but, at the same time, did not want to stay at the hotel too long. So, the party had to be after two days and all the people in the city were handed over the invitations personally. Joint secretary Satyapalan's invitation was given to his secretary but they were advised to include director Jag Mohan Gupta and his wife. Gupta received Joshi and Rohatgi respectfully and said that the Japanese investment was particularly welcome. There was no hint or suggestion of money. Actually they were treated as belonging to a select group.

Muni Lal phoned the Kapoors and asked them to come. Kuldip replied that he could come alone. Muni Lal asked him to come by train as on the journey back he could go in Muni Lal's car. Kapoor made a condition. From Chandigarh they would have to go to Ludhiana. Muni Lal agreed as after all his daughter and her husband were there. Then Kapoor not only congratulated Muni Lal on the success regarding the Japanese project but also disclosed that his daughter's marriage negotiations could be said to be successful. It was in this connection, to sort out details, he was going to Ludhiana. He was thankful to Muni Lal and his wife.

A room was hired in the hotel for the evening. The three Indians worked out menus of vegetarian and non-vegetarian. food. A difficulty arose about drinks. Watanabe group wanted to buy them at a reasonable rate from the market. The hotel insisted that all supplies would have to come from the hotel at its official rate. A compromise was arrived at. The group ordered small quantity of whisky, gin and beer and soft drinks. The rest they collected surreptitiously from the bazaar. The hotel people kept mentioning that what had been asked for was too little. These people were told that they would be asked to supply more at the time when the shortage occurred. Kapoor arrived in good time and quietly became part of the reception group. But slowly they grew anxious. Until 20 minutes after the official start of the party, nobody has arrived. Only Kapoor kept encouraging them by saying that it was a usual style.

The first to arrive was Kashiji, who used to run the state branch office in New Delhi. He kept telling everybody that he just happened to be in Chandigarh and Joshi had run into him. Kashiji could not absent himself from such a joyous occasion. People did turn up in due course of time. The Joint Secretary could not make it but the director did with his confident looking wife. Dayal Singh came in his native dress. Muni Lal was particularly happy to see him as otherwise a person like Joshi might think he did not exist. Dayal Singh was without his wife but his son, or one of his sons, as he pointed out, accompanied him, Dayal Singh showed no objection to alcohol. The son touched Watanabe's feet, Indian style greeting to important people, and kept informing everybody that he could help in settling any official matters. He distributed his name cards judiciously. Dayal Singh said that he was quite sure that things would work out well. It was quietly mentioned that no extra expenditure was involved. All people were worldly wise and avoided claiming that theirs was the only such case. Dayal Singh said that the job was not over. Land had to be selected and possession certificate obtained. The land allotted had to be measured and neighbouring villagers to be placated. They were bound to say that part of their land had been wrongly handed over to the Japanese but they could be dealt with reasonably. Somebody might be sitting on the land growing vegetables in a patch. He would need to be negotiated with. Dayal Singh said that work of recruitment of labour for the factory was still away as the factory had to be built and stocked. Brigadier Vishwanathan and his wife were popular. The Brigadier and Kapoor got together well. Party became very cheerful as quite a few people, not known to the hosts were present and helping themselves seriously. Madan Mohan and Maheshwari, now a minister, did not come for political reasons.

Kapoor emphasized that Muni Lal was a person of virtuous life and he must have acted virtuously in his previous life. In this very month, he helped in acquisition of land for the Japanese project and helped him in settling his daughter's marriage. Muni Lal, he said, was like a brother to him.

The hardcore stayed late at the party. Kapoor being experienced of such functions, suggested quietly to Watanabe that he could absent himself.

□□□

BUNNER SISTERS

Edith Wharton

HAWK PRESS

Published by

Hawk Press
4836/24, Ansari Road, Daryaganj
New Delhi – 110 002
Phones : 9643330713, 91-11-23278618, 91-11-35676207
E-mail: thehawkpress@gmail.com
www.thehawkpress.com

ISBN : 978-93-92322-01-3

CONTENTS

Part-I

Part-II

PART-I

CHAPTER I

In the days when New York's traffic moved at the pace of the drooping horse-car, when society applauded Christine Nilsson at the Academy of Music and basked in the sunsets of the Hudson River School on the walls of the National Academy of Design, an inconspicuous shop with a single show-window was intimately and favourably known to the feminine population of the quarter bordering on Stuyvesant Square.

It was a very small shop, in a shabby basement, in a side-street already doomed to decline; and from the miscellaneous display behind the window-pane, and the brevity of the sign surmounting it (merely "Bunner Sisters" in blotchy gold on a black ground) it would have been difficult for the uninitiated to guess the precise nature of the business carried on within. But that was of little consequence, since its fame was so purely local that the customers on whom its existence depended were almost congenitally aware of the exact range of "goods" to be found at Bunner Sisters'.

The house of which Bunner Sisters had annexed the basement was a private dwelling with a brick front, green shutters on weak hinges, and a dress-maker's sign in the window above the shop. On each side of its modest three stories stood higher buildings, with fronts of brown stone, cracked and blistered, cast-iron balconies and cat-haunted grass-patches behind twisted railings. These houses too had once been private, but now a cheap lunchroom filled the basement of one, while the other announced itself, above the knotty wistaria that clasped its central balcony, as the Mendoza Family Hotel. It was obvious from the chronic cluster of refuse-barrels at its area-gate and the blurred surface of its curtainless windows, that the families frequenting the Mendoza

Hotel were not exacting in their tastes; though they doubtless indulged in as much fastidiousness as they could afford to pay for, and rather more than their landlord thought they had a right to express.

These three houses fairly exemplified the general character of the street, which, as it stretched eastward, rapidly fell from shabbiness to squalor, with an increasing frequency of projecting sign-boards, and of swinging doors that softly shut or opened at the touch of red-nosed men and pale little girls with broken jugs. The middle of the street was full of irregular depressions, well adapted to retain the long swirls of dust and straw and twisted paper that the wind drove up and down its sad untended length; and toward the end of the day, when traffic had been active, the fissured pavement formed a mosaic of coloured hand-bills, lids of tomato-cans, old shoes, cigar-stumps and banana skins, cemented together by a layer of mud, or veiled in a powdering of dust, as the state of the weather determined.

The sole refuge offered from the contemplation of this depressing waste was the sight of the Bunner Sisters' window. Its panes were always well-washed, and though their display of artificial flowers, bands of scalloped flannel, wire hat-frames, and jars of home-made preserves, had the undefinable greyish tinge of objects long preserved in the show-case of a museum, the window revealed a background of orderly counters and white-washed walls in pleasant contrast to the adjoining dinginess.

The Bunner sisters were proud of the neatness of their shop and content with its humble prosperity. It was not what they had once imagined it would be, but though it presented but a shrunken image of their earlier ambitions it enabled them to pay their rent and keep themselves alive and out of debt; and it was long since their hopes had soared higher.

Now and then, however, among their greyer hours there came one not bright enough to be called sunny, but rather of the silvery twilight hue which sometimes ends a day of storm. It was such an hour that Ann Eliza, the elder of the firm, was soberly enjoying as she sat one January evening in the back room which served as bedroom, kitchen and parlour to herself and her sister Evelina. In the shop the blinds had been drawn down, the counters cleared and the wares in the window lightly covered with an old sheet; but the shop-door remained unlocked till Evelina, who had taken a parcel to the dyer's, should come back.

In the back room a kettle bubbled on the stove, and Ann Eliza had laid a cloth over one end of the centre table, and placed near the green-shaded sewing lamp two tea-cups, two plates, a sugar-bowl and a piece of pie. The rest of the room remained in a greenish shadow which discreetly veiled the outline of an old-fashioned mahogany bedstead surmounted by a chromo of a young lady in a night-gown who clung with eloquently-rolling eyes to a crag described in illuminated letters as the Rock of Ages; and against the unshaded windows two rocking-chairs and a sewing-machine were silhouetted on the dusk.

Ann Eliza, her small and habitually anxious face smoothed to unusual serenity, and the streaks of pale hair on her veined temples shining glossily beneath the lamp, had seated herself at the table, and was tying up, with her usual fumbling deliberation, a knobby object wrapped in paper. Now and then, as she struggled with the string, which was too short, she fancied she heard the click of the shop-door, and paused to listen for her sister; then, as no one came, she straightened her spectacles and entered into renewed conflict with the parcel. In honour of some event of obvious importance, she had put on her double-dyed and triple-turned black silk. Age, while bestowing on this garment a patine worthy of a Renaissance bronze, had deprived it of whatever curves the wearer's pre-Raphaelite figure had once been able to impress on it; but this stiffness of outline gave it an air of sacerdotal state which seemed to emphasize the importance of the occasion.

Seen thus, in her sacramental black silk, a wisp of lace turned over the collar and fastened by a mosaic brooch, and her face smoothed into harmony with her apparel, Ann Eliza looked ten years younger than behind the counter, in the heat and burden of the day. It would have been as difficult to guess her approximate age as that of the black silk, for she had the same worn and glossy aspect as her dress; but a faint tinge of pink still lingered on her cheek-bones, like the reflection of sunset which sometimes colours the west long after the day is over.

When she had tied the parcel to her satisfaction, and laid it with furtive accuracy just opposite her sister's plate, she sat down, with an air of obviously-assumed indifference, in one of the rocking-chairs near the window; and a moment later the shop-door opened and Evelina entered.

The younger Bunner sister, who was a little taller than her elder, had a more pronounced nose, but a weaker slope of mouth and chin. She still permitted herself the frivolity of waving her pale hair, and its tight little ridges, stiff as the tresses of an Assyrian statue, were flattened under a dotted veil which ended at the tip of her cold-reddened nose. In her scant jacket and skirt of black cashmere she looked singularly nipped and faded; but it seemed possible that under happier conditions she might still warm into relative youth.

"Why, Ann Eliza," she exclaimed, in a thin voice pitched to chronic fretfulness, "what in the world you got your best silk on for?"

Ann Eliza had risen with a blush that made her steel-browed spectacles incongruous.

"Why, Evelina, why shouldn't I, I sh'ld like to know? Ain't it your birthday, dear?" She put out her arms with the awkwardness of habitually repressed emotion.

Evelina, without seeming to notice the gesture, threw back the jacket from her narrow shoulders.

"Oh, pshaw," she said, less peevishly. "I guess we'd better give up birthdays. Much as we can do to keep Christmas nowadays."

"You hadn't oughter say that, Evelina. We ain't so badly off as all that. I guess you're cold and tired. Set down while I take the kettle off: it's right on the boil."

She pushed Evelina toward the table, keeping a sideward eye on her sister's listless movements, while her own hands were busy with the kettle. A moment later came the exclamation for which she waited.

"Why, Ann Eliza!" Evelina stood transfixed by the sight of the parcel beside her plate.

Ann Eliza, tremulously engaged in filling the teapot, lifted a look of hypocritical surprise.

"Sakes, Evelina! What's the matter?"

The younger sister had rapidly untied the string, and drawn from its wrappings a round nickel clock of the kind to be bought for a dollar-seventy-five.

"Oh, Ann Eliza, how could you?" She set the clock down, and the sisters exchanged agitated glances across the table.

"Well," the elder retorted, "*Ain't* it your birthday?"

"Yes, but—"

"Well, and ain't you had to run round the corner to the Square every morning, rain or shine, to see what time it was, ever since we had to sell mother's watch last July? Ain't you, Evelina?"

"Yes, but—"

"There ain't any buts. We've always wanted a clock and now we've got one: that's all there is about it. Ain't she a beauty, Evelina?" Ann Eliza, putting back the kettle on the stove, leaned over her sister's shoulder to pass an approving hand over the circular rim of the clock. "Hear how loud she ticks. I was afraid you'd hear her soon as you come in."

"No. I wasn't thinking," murmured Evelina.

"Well, ain't you glad now?" Ann Eliza gently reproached her. The rebuke had no acerbity, for she knew that Evelina's seeming indifference was alive with unexpressed scruples.

"I'm real glad, sister; but you hadn't oughter. We could have got on well enough without."

"Evelina Bunner, just you sit down to your tea. I guess I know what I'd oughter and what I'd hadn't oughter just as well as you do—I'm old enough!"

"You're real good, Ann Eliza; but I know you've given up something you needed to get me this clock."

"What do I need, I'd like to know? Ain't I got a best black silk?" the elder sister said with a laugh full of nervous pleasure.

She poured out Evelina's tea, adding some condensed milk from the jug, and cutting for her the largest slice of pie; then she drew up her own chair to the table.

The two women ate in silence for a few moments before Evelina began to speak again. "The clock is perfectly lovely and I don't say it ain't a comfort to have it; but I hate to think what it must have cost you."

"No, it didn't, neither," Ann Eliza retorted. "I got it dirt cheap, if you want to know. And I paid for it out of a little extra work I did the other night on the machine for Mrs. Hawkins."

"The baby-waists?"

"Yes."

"There, I knew it! You swore to me you'd buy a new pair of shoes with that money."

"Well, and s'posin' I didn't want 'em—what then? I've patched up the old ones as good as new—and I do declare, Evelina Bunner, if you ask me another question you'll go and spoil all my pleasure."

"Very well, I won't," said the younger sister.

They continued to eat without farther words. Evelina yielded to her sister's entreaty that she should finish the pie, and poured out a second cup of tea, into which she put the last lump of sugar; and between them, on the table, the clock kept up its sociable tick.

"Where'd you get it, Ann Eliza?" asked Evelina, fascinated.

"Where'd you s'pose? Why, right round here, over acrost the Square, in the queerest little store you ever laid eyes on. I saw it in the window as I was passing, and I stepped right in and asked how much it was, and the store-keeper he was real pleasant about it. He was just the nicest man. I guess he's a German. I told him I couldn't give much, and he said, well, he knew what hard times was too. His name's Ramy—Herman Ramy: I saw it written up over the store. And he told me he used to work at Tiff'ny's, oh, for years, in the clock-department, and three years ago he took sick with some kinder fever, and lost his place, and when he got well they'd engaged somebody else and didn't want him, and so he started this little store by himself. I guess he's real smart, and he spoke quite like an educated man—but he looks sick."

Evelina was listening with absorbed attention. In the narrow lives of the two sisters such an episode was not to be under-rated.

"What you say his name was?" she asked as Ann Eliza paused.

"Herman Ramy."

"How old is he?"

"Well, I couldn't exactly tell you, he looked so sick—but I don't b'lieve he's much over forty."

By this time the plates had been cleared and the teapot emptied, and the two sisters rose from the table. Ann Eliza, tying an apron over her black silk, carefully removed all traces of the meal; then, after washing the cups and plates, and putting them away in a cupboard, she drew her rocking-chair to the lamp and sat down to a heap of mending. Evelina, meanwhile, had been roaming about the room in search of an abiding-place for the clock. A rosewood what-not with ornamental fret-work hung on the wall beside the devout young lady in dishabille, and after much weighing of alternatives the sisters decided to dethrone a broken china vase filled with dried grasses which had long stood on the top shelf, and to put the clock in its place; the vase, after farther consideration, being relegated to a small table covered with blue and white beadwork, which held a Bible and prayer-book, and an illustrated copy of Longfellow's poems given as a school-prize to their father.

This change having been made, and the effect studied from every angle of the room, Evelina languidly put her pinking-machine on the table, and sat down to the monotonous work of pinking a heap of black silk flounces. The strips of stuff slid slowly to the floor at her side, and the clock, from its commanding altitude, kept time with the dispiriting click of the instrument under her fingers.

CHAPTER II

The purchase of Evelina's clock had been a more important event in the life of Ann Eliza Bunner than her younger sister could divine. In the first place, there had been the demoralizing satisfaction of finding herself in possession of a sum of money which she need not put into the common fund, but could spend as she chose, without consulting Evelina, and then the excitement of her stealthy trips abroad, undertaken on the rare occasions when she could trump up a pretext for leaving the shop; since, as a rule, it was Evelina who took the bundles to the dyer's, and delivered the purchases of those among their customers who were too genteel to be seen carrying home a bonnet or a bundle of pinking—so that, had it not been for the excuse of having to see Mrs. Hawkins's teething baby, Ann Eliza would hardly have known what motive to allege for deserting her usual seat behind the counter.

The infrequency of her walks made them the chief events of her life. The mere act of going out from the monastic quiet of the shop into the tumult of the streets filled her with a subdued excitement which grew too intense for pleasure as she was swallowed by the engulfing roar of Broadway or Third Avenue, and began to do timid battle with their incessant cross-currents of humanity. After a glance or two into the great show-windows she usually allowed herself to be swept back into the shelter of a side-street, and finally regained her own roof in a state of breathless bewilderment and fatigue; but gradually, as her nerves were soothed by the familiar quiet of the little shop, and the click of Evelina's pinking-machine, certain sights and sounds would detach themselves from the torrent along which she had been swept, and she would devote the rest of the day to a mental reconstruction of the different episodes of her walk, till finally it took shape in her thought as a consecutive and highly-coloured experience, from which, for weeks afterwards, she would detach some fragmentary recollection in the course of her long dialogues with her sister.

But when, to the unwonted excitement of going out, was added the intenser interest of looking for a present for Evelina, Ann Eliza's agitation, sharpened by concealment, actually preyed upon her rest; and it was not till the present had been given, and she had unbosomed herself of the experiences connected with its purchase, that she could look back with anything like composure to that stirring moment of her life. From that day forward, however, she began to take a certain tranquil pleasure in thinking of Mr. Ramy's small shop, not unlike her own in its countrified obscurity, though the layer of dust which covered its counter and shelves made the comparison only superficially acceptable. Still, she did not judge the state of the shop severely, for Mr. Ramy had told her that he was alone in the world, and lone men, she was aware, did not know how to deal with dust. It gave her a good deal of occupation to wonder why he had never married, or if, on the other hand, he were a widower, and had lost all his dear little children; and she scarcely knew which alternative seemed to make him the more interesting. In either case, his life was assuredly a sad one; and she passed many hours in speculating on the manner in which he probably spent his evenings. She knew he lived at the back of his shop, for she had caught, on entering, a glimpse of a dingy room with a tumbled bed; and the pervading smell of cold fry suggested that he probably did his own cooking. She wondered if he did not often make his tea with water that had not boiled, and asked herself, almost jealously, who looked after the shop while he went to market. Then it occurred to her as likely that he bought his provisions at the same market as Evelina; and she was fascinated by the thought that he and her sister might constantly be meeting in total unconsciousness of the link between them. Whenever she reached this stage in her reflexions she lifted a furtive glance to the clock, whose loud staccato tick was becoming a part of her inmost being.

The seed sown by these long hours of meditation germinated at last in the secret wish to go to market some morning in Evelina's stead. As this purpose rose to the surface of Ann Eliza's thoughts she shrank back shyly from its contemplation. A plan so steeped in duplicity had never before taken shape in her crystalline soul. How was it possible for her to consider such a step? And, besides, (she did not possess sufficient logic to mark the downward trend of this "besides"), what excuse could she make that would not excite her sister's curiosity? From this second query it was an easy descent to the third: how soon could she manage to go?

It was Evelina herself, who furnished the necessary pretext by awaking with a sore throat on the day when she usually went to market. It was a Saturday, and as they always had their bit of steak on Sunday the expedition could not be postponed, and it seemed natural that Ann Eliza, as she tied an old stocking around Evelina's throat, should announce her intention of stepping round to the butcher's.

"Oh, Ann Eliza, they'll cheat you so," her sister wailed.

Ann Eliza brushed aside the imputation with a smile, and a few minutes later, having set the room to rights, and cast a last glance at the shop, she was tying on her bonnet with fumbling haste.

The morning was damp and cold, with a sky full of sulky clouds that would not make room for the sun, but as yet dropped only an occasional snow-flake. In the early light the street looked its meanest and most neglected; but to Ann Eliza, never greatly troubled by any untidiness for which she was not responsible, it seemed to wear a singularly friendly aspect.

A few minutes' walk brought her to the market where Evelina made her purchases, and where, if he had any sense of topographical fitness, Mr. Ramy must also deal.

Ann Eliza, making her way through the outskirts of potato-barrels and flabby fish, found no one in the shop but the gory-aproned butcher who stood in the background cutting chops.

As she approached him across the tesselation of fish-scales, blood and saw-dust, he laid aside his cleaver and not unsympathetically asked: “Sister sick?”

“Oh, not very—jest a cold,” she answered, as guiltily as if Evelina's illness had been feigned. “We want a steak as usual, please—and my sister said you was to be sure to give me jest as good a cut as if it was her,” she added with child-like candour.

“Oh, that's all right.” The butcher picked up his weapon with a grin. “Your sister knows a cut as well as any of us,” he remarked.

In another moment, Ann Eliza reflected, the steak would be cut and wrapped up, and no choice left her but to turn her disappointed steps toward home. She was too shy to try to delay the butcher by such conversational arts as she possessed, but the approach of a deaf old lady in an antiquated bonnet and mantle gave her her opportunity.

“Wait on her first, please,” Ann Eliza whispered. “I ain't in any hurry.”

The butcher advanced to his new customer, and Ann Eliza, palpitating in the back of the shop, saw that the old lady's hesitations between liver and pork chops were likely to be indefinitely prolonged. They were still unresolved when she was interrupted by the entrance of a blowsy Irish girl with a basket on her arm. The newcomer caused a momentary diversion, and when she had departed the old lady, who was evidently as intolerant of interruption as a professional story-teller, insisted on returning to the beginning of her complicated order, and weighing anew, with an anxious appeal to the butcher's arbitration, the relative advantages of pork and liver. But even her hesitations, and the intrusion on them of two or three other customers, were of no avail, for Mr. Ramy was not among those who entered the shop; and at last Ann Eliza, ashamed of staying longer, reluctantly claimed her steak, and walked home through the thickening snow.

Even to her simple judgment the vanity of her hopes was plain, and in the clear light that disappointment turns upon our actions she wondered how she could have been foolish enough to suppose that, even if Mr. Ramy *did* go to that particular market, he would hit on the same day and hour as herself.

There followed a colourless week unmarked by farther incident. The old stocking cured Evelina's throat, and Mrs. Hawkins dropped in once or twice to talk of her baby's teeth; some new orders for pinking were received, and Evelina sold a bonnet to the lady with puffed sleeves. The lady with puffed sleeves—a resident of "the Square," whose name they had never learned, because she always carried her own parcels home—was the most distinguished and interesting figure on their horizon. She was youngish, she was elegant (as the title they had given her implied), and she had a sweet sad smile about which they had woven many histories; but even the news of her return to town—it was her first apparition that year—failed to arouse Ann Eliza's interest. All the small daily happenings which had once sufficed to fill the hours now appeared to her in their deadly insignificance; and for the first time in her long years of drudgery she rebelled at the dullness of her life. With Evelina such fits of discontent were habitual and openly proclaimed, and Ann Eliza still excused them as one of the prerogatives of youth. Besides, Evelina had not been intended by Providence to pine in such a narrow life: in the original plan of things, she had been meant to marry and have a baby, to wear silk on Sundays, and take a leading part in a Church circle. Hitherto opportunity had played her false; and for all her superior aspirations and carefully crimped hair she had remained as obscure and unsought as Ann Eliza. But the elder sister, who had long since accepted her own fate, had never accepted Evelina's. Once a pleasant young man who taught in Sunday-school had paid the younger Miss Bunner a few shy visits. That was years since, and he had speedily vanished from their view. Whether he had carried with him any of Evelina's illusions, Ann Eliza had never discovered; but his attentions had clad her sister in a halo of exquisite possibilities.

Ann Eliza, in those days, had never dreamed of allowing herself the luxury of self-pity: it seemed as much a personal right of Evelina's as her elaborately crinkled hair. But now she began to transfer to herself a portion of the sympathy she had so long bestowed on Evelina. She had at last recognized her right to set up some lost opportunities of her own; and once that dangerous precedent established, they began to crowd upon her memory.

It was at this stage of Ann Eliza's transformation that Evelina, looking up one evening from her work, said suddenly: "My! She's stopped."

Ann Eliza, raising her eyes from a brown merino seam, followed her sister's glance across the room. It was a Monday, and they always wound the clock on Sundays.

"Are you sure you wound her yesterday, Evelina?"

"Jest as sure as I live. She must be broke. I'll go and see."

Evelina laid down the hat she was trimming, and took the clock from its shelf.

"There—I knew it! She's wound jest as *tight*—what you suppose's happened to her, Ann Eliza?"

"I dunno, I'm sure," said the elder sister, wiping her spectacles before proceeding to a close examination of the clock.

With anxiously bent heads the two women shook and turned it, as though they were trying to revive a living thing; but it remained unresponsive to their touch, and at length Evelina laid it down with a sigh.

"Seems like somethin' *dead*, don't it, Ann Eliza? How still the room is!"

"Yes, ain't it?"

"Well, I'll put her back where she belongs," Evelina continued, in the tone of one about to perform the last offices for the departed. "And I guess," she added, "you'll have to step round to Mr. Ramy's to-morrow, and see if he can fix her."

Ann Eliza's face burned. "I—yes, I guess I'll have to," she stammered, stooping to pick up a spool of cotton which had rolled to the floor. A sudden heart-throb stretched the seams of her flat alpaca bosom, and a pulse leapt to life in each of her temples.

That night, long after Evelina slept, Ann Eliza lay awake in the unfamiliar silence, more acutely conscious of the nearness of the crippled clock than when it had volubly told out the minutes. The next morning she woke from a troubled dream of having carried it to Mr. Ramy's, and found that he and his shop had vanished; and all through the day's occupations the memory of this dream oppressed her.

It had been agreed that Ann Eliza should take the clock to be repaired as soon as they had dined; but while they were still at table a weak-eyed little girl in a black apron stabbed with innumerable pins burst in on them with the cry: "Oh, Miss Bunner, for mercy's sake! Miss Mellins has been took again."

Miss Mellins was the dress-maker upstairs, and the weak-eyed child one of her youthful apprentices.

Ann Eliza started from her seat. "I'll come at once. Quick, Evelina, the cordial!"

By this euphemistic name the sisters designated a bottle of cherry brandy, the last of a dozen inherited from their grandmother, which they kept locked in their cupboard against such emergencies. A moment later, cordial in hand, Ann Eliza was hurrying upstairs behind the weak-eyed child.

Miss Mellins' "turn" was sufficiently serious to detain Ann Eliza for nearly two hours, and dusk had fallen when she took up the depleted bottle of cordial and descended again to the shop. It was empty, as usual, and Evelina sat at her pinking-machine in the back room. Ann Eliza was still agitated by her efforts to restore the dress-maker, but in spite of her preoccupation she was struck, as soon as she entered, by the loud tick of the clock, which still stood on the shelf where she had left it.

"Why, she's going!" she gasped, before Evelina could question her about Miss Mellins. "Did she start up again by herself?"

"Oh, no; but I couldn't stand not knowing what time it was, I've got so accustomed to having her round; and just after you went upstairs Mrs. Hawkins dropped in, so I asked her to tend the store for a minute, and I clapped on my things and ran right round to Mr. Ramy's. It turned out there wasn't anything the matter with her—nothin' on'y a speck of dust in the works—and he fixed her for me in a minute and I brought her right back. Ain't it lovely to hear her going again? But tell me about Miss Mellins, quick!"

For a moment Ann Eliza found no words. Not till she learned that she had missed her chance did she understand how many hopes had hung upon it. Even now she did not know why she had wanted so much to see the clock-maker again.

"I s'pose it's because nothing's ever happened to me," she thought, with a twinge of envy for the fate which gave Evelina every opportunity that came their way. "She had the Sunday-school teacher too," Ann Eliza murmured to herself; but she was well-trained in the arts of renunciation, and after a scarcely perceptible pause she plunged into a detailed description of the dress-maker's "turn."

Evelina, when her curiosity was roused, was an insatiable questioner, and it was supper-time before she had come to the end of her enquiries about Miss Mellins; but when the two sisters had seated themselves at their evening meal Ann Eliza at last found a chance to say: "So she on'y had a speck of dust in her."

Evelina understood at once that the reference was not to Miss Mellins. "Yes—at least he thinks so," she answered, helping herself as a matter of course to the first cup of tea.

"On'y to think!" murmured Ann Eliza.

"But he isn't *sure*," Evelina continued, absently pushing the teapot toward her sister. "It may be something wrong with the—I forget what he called it. Anyhow, he said he'd call round and see, day after to-morrow, after supper."

"Who said?" gasped Ann Eliza.

"Why, Mr. Ramy, of course. I think he's real nice, Ann Eliza. And I don't believe he's forty; but he *does* look sick. I guess he's pretty lonesome, all by himself in that store. He as much as told me so, and somehow"—Evelina paused and bridled—"I kinder thought that maybe his saying he'd call round about the clock was on'y just an excuse. He said it just as I was going out of the store. What you think, Ann Eliza?"

"Oh, I don't har'ly know." To save herself, Ann Eliza could produce nothing warmer.

"Well, I don't pretend to be smarter than other folks," said Evelina, putting a conscious hand to her hair, "but I guess Mr. Herman Ramy wouldn't be sorry to pass an evening here, 'stead of spending it all alone in that poky little place of his."

Her self-consciousness irritated Ann Eliza.

"I guess he's got plenty of friends of his own," she said, almost harshly.

"No, he ain't, either. He's got hardly any."

"Did he tell you that too?" Even to her own ears there was a faint sneer in the interrogation.

"Yes, he did," said Evelina, dropping her lids with a smile. "He seemed to be just crazy to talk to somebody—somebody agreeable, I mean. I think the man's unhappy, Ann Eliza."

"So do I," broke from the elder sister.

"He seems such an educated man, too. He was reading the paper when I went in. Ain't it sad to think of his being reduced to that little store, after being years at Tiff'ny's, and one of the head men in their clock-department?"

"He told you all that?"

"Why, yes. I think he'd a' told me everything ever happened to him if I'd had the time to stay and listen. I tell you he's dead lonely, Ann Eliza."

"Yes," said Ann Eliza.

CHAPTER III

Two days afterward, Ann Eliza noticed that Evelina, before they sat down to supper, pinned a crimson bow under her collar; and when the meal was finished the younger sister, who seldom concerned herself with the clearing of the table, set about with nervous haste to help Ann Eliza in the removal of the dishes.

"I hate to see food mussing about," she grumbled. "Ain't it hateful having to do everything in one room?"

"Oh, Evelina, I've always thought we was so comfortable," Ann Eliza protested.

"Well, so we are, comfortable enough; but I don't suppose there's any harm in my saying I wisht we had a parlour, is there? Anyway, we might manage to buy a screen to hide the bed."

Ann Eliza coloured. There was something vaguely embarrassing in Evelina's suggestion.

"I always think if we ask for more what we have may be taken from us," she ventured.

"Well, whoever took it wouldn't get much," Evelina retorted with a laugh as she swept up the table-cloth.

A few moments later the back room was in its usual flawless order and the two sisters had seated themselves near the lamp. Ann Eliza had taken up her sewing, and Evelina was preparing to make artificial flowers. The sisters usually relegated this more delicate business to the long leisure of the summer months; but to-night Evelina had brought out the box which lay all winter under the bed, and spread before her a bright array of muslin petals, yellow stamens and green corollas, and a tray of little implements curiously suggestive of the dental art. Ann Eliza made no remark on this unusual proceeding; perhaps she guessed why, for that evening her sister had chosen a graceful task.

Presently a knock on the outer door made them look up; but Evelina, the first on her feet, said promptly: "Sit still. I'll see who it is."

Ann Eliza was glad to sit still: the baby's petticoat that she was stitching shook in her fingers.

"Sister, here's Mr. Ramy come to look at the clock," said Evelina, a moment later, in the high drawl she cultivated before strangers; and a shortish man with a pale bearded face and upturned coat-collar came stiffly into the room.

Ann Eliza let her work fall as she stood up. "You're very welcome, I'm sure, Mr. Ramy. It's real kind of you to call."

"Nod ad all, ma'am." A tendency to illustrate Grimm's law in the interchange of his consonants betrayed the clockmaker's nationality, but he was evidently used to speaking English, or at least the particular branch of the vernacular with which the Bunner sisters were familiar. "I don't like to led any clock go out of my store without being sure it gives satisfaction," he added.

"Oh—but we were satisfied," Ann Eliza assured him.

"But I wasn't, you see, ma'am," said Mr. Ramy looking slowly about the room, "nor I won't be, not till I see that clock's going all right."

"May I assist you off with your coat, Mr. Ramy?" Evelina interposed. She could never trust Ann Eliza to remember these opening ceremonies.

"Thank you, ma'am," he replied, and taking his thread-bare over-coat and shabby hat she laid them on a chair with the gesture she imagined the lady with the puffed sleeves might make use of on similar occasions. Ann Eliza's social sense was roused, and she felt that the next act of hospitality must be hers. "Won't you suit yourself to a seat?" she suggested. "My sister will reach down the clock; but I'm sure she's all right again. She's went beautiful ever since you fixed her."

"Dat's good," said Mr. Ramy. His lips parted in a smile which showed a row of yellowish teeth with one or two gaps in it; but in spite of this disclosure Ann Eliza thought his smile extremely pleasant: there was something wistful and conciliating in it which agreed with the pathos of his sunken cheeks and prominent eyes. As he took the lamp, the light fell on his bulging forehead and wide skull thinly covered with grayish hair. His hands were pale and broad, with knotty joints and square finger-tips rimmed with grime; but his touch was as light as a woman's.

"Well, ladies, dat clock's all right," he pronounced.

"I'm sure we're very much obliged to you," said Evelina, throwing a glance at her sister.

"Oh," Ann Eliza murmured, involuntarily answering the admonition. She selected a key from the bunch that hung at her waist with her cutting-out scissors, and fitting it into the lock of the cupboard, brought out the cherry brandy and three old-fashioned glasses engraved with vine-wreaths.

"It's a very cold night," she said, "and maybe you'd like a sip of this cordial. It was made a great while ago by our grandmother."

"It looks fine," said Mr. Ramy bowing, and Ann Eliza filled the glasses. In her own and Evelina's she poured only a few drops, but she filled their guest's to the brim. "My sister and I seldom take wine," she explained.

With another bow, which included both his hostesses, Mr. Ramy drank off the cherry brandy and pronounced it excellent.

Evelina meanwhile, with an assumption of industry intended to put their guest at ease, had taken up her instruments and was twisting a rose-petal into shape.

"You make artificial flowers, I see, ma'am," said Mr. Ramy with interest. "It's very pretty work. I had a lady-vriend in Shermany dat used to make flowers." He put out a square finger-tip to touch the petal.

Evelina blushed a little. "You left Germany long ago, I suppose?"

"Dear me yes, a goot while ago. I was only ninedeen when I come to the States."

After this the conversation dragged on intermittently till Mr. Ramy, peering about the room with the short-sighted glance of his race, said with an air of interest: "You're pleasantly fixed here; it looks real cosy." The note of wistfulness in his voice was obscurely moving to Ann Eliza.

"Oh, we live very plainly," said Evelina, with an affectation of grandeur deeply impressive to her sister. "We have very simple tastes."

"You look real comfortable, anyhow," said Mr. Ramy. His bulging eyes seemed to muster the details of the scene with a gentle envy. "I wisht I had as good a store; but I guess no blace seems home-like when you're always alone in it."

For some minutes longer the conversation moved on at this desultory pace, and then Mr. Ramy, who had been obviously nerving himself for the difficult act of departure, took his leave with an abruptness which would have startled anyone used to the subtler gradations of intercourse. But to Ann Eliza and her sister there was nothing surprising in his abrupt retreat. The long-drawn agonies of preparing to leave, and the subsequent dumb plunge through the door, were so usual in their circle that they would have been as much embarrassed as Mr. Ramy if he had tried to put any fluency into his adieux.

After he had left both sisters remained silent for a while; then Evelina, laying aside her unfinished flower, said: "I'll go and lock up."

CHAPTER IV

Intolerably monotonous seemed now to the Bunner sisters the treadmill routine of the shop, colourless and long their evenings about the lamp, aimless their habitual interchange of words to the weary accompaniment of the sewing and pinking machines.

It was perhaps with the idea of relieving the tension of their mood that Evelina, the following Sunday, suggested inviting Miss Mellins to supper. The Bunner sisters were not in a position to be lavish of the humblest hospitality, but two or three times in the year they shared their evening meal with a friend; and Miss Mellins, still flushed with the importance of her "turn," seemed the most interesting guest they could invite.

As the three women seated themselves at the supper-table, embellished by the unwonted addition of pound cake and sweet pickles, the dress-maker's sharp swarthy person stood out vividly between the neutral-tinted sisters. Miss Mellins was a small woman with a glossy yellow face and a frizz of black hair bristling with imitation tortoise-shell pins. Her sleeves had a fashionable cut, and half a dozen metal bangles rattled on her wrists. Her voice rattled like her bangles as she poured forth a stream of anecdote and ejaculation; and her round black eyes jumped with acrobatic velocity from one face to another. Miss Mellins was always having or hearing of amazing adventures. She had surprised a burglar in her room at midnight (though how he got there, what he robbed her of, and by what means he escaped had never been quite clear to her auditors); she had been warned by anonymous letters that her grocer (a rejected suitor) was putting poison in her tea; she had a customer who was shadowed by detectives, and another (a very wealthy lady) who had been arrested in a department store for kleptomania; she had been present at a spiritualist seance where an old gentleman had died in a fit on seeing a materialization of his mother-in-law; she had escaped from two fires in her night-gown, and at the funeral of her first cousin the horses attached to the hearse had run away and smashed the coffin, precipitating her relative into an open man-hole before the eyes of his distracted family.

A sceptical observer might have explained Miss Mellins's proneness to adventure by the fact that she derived her chief mental nourishment from the Police Gazette and the Fireside Weekly; but her lot was cast in a circle where such insinuations were not likely to be heard, and where the title-role in blood-curdling drama had long been her recognized right.

"Yes," she was now saying, her emphatic eyes on Ann Eliza, "you may not believe it, Miss Bunner, and I don't know's I should myself if anybody else was to tell me, but over a year before ever I was born, my mother she went to see a gypsy fortune-teller that was exhibited in a tent on the Battery with the green-headed lady, though her father warned her not to—and what you s'pose she told her? Why, she told her these very words—says she: 'Your next child'll be a girl with jet-black curls, and she'll suffer from spasms.'"

"Mercy!" murmured Ann Eliza, a ripple of sympathy running down her spine.

"D'you ever have spasms before, Miss Mellins?" Evelina asked.

"Yes, ma'am," the dress-maker declared. "And where'd you suppose I had 'em? Why, at my cousin Emma McIntyre's wedding, her that married the apothecary over in Jersey City, though her mother appeared to her in a dream and told her she'd rue the day she done it, but as Emma said, she got more advice than she wanted from the living, and if she was to listen to spectres too she'd never be sure what she'd ought to do and what she'd oughtn't; but I will say her husband took to drink, and she never was the same woman after her fust baby—well, they had an elegant church wedding, and what you s'pose I saw as I was walkin' up the aisle with the wedding percession?"

"Well?" Ann Eliza whispered, forgetting to thread her needle.

"Why, a coffin, to be sure, right on the top step of the chancel—Emma's folks is 'piscopalians and she would have a church wedding, though *his* mother raised a terrible rumpus over it—well, there it set, right in front of where the minister stood that was going to marry 'em, a coffin covered with a black velvet pall with a gold fringe, and a 'Gates Ajar' in white camellias atop of it."

"Goodness," said Evelina, starting, "there's a knock!"

"Who can it be?" shuddered Ann Eliza, still under the spell of Miss Mellins's hallucination.

Evelina rose and lit a candle to guide her through the shop. They heard her turn the key of the outer door, and a gust of night air stirred the close atmosphere of the back room; then there was a sound of vivacious exclamations, and Evelina returned with Mr. Ramy.

Ann Eliza's heart rocked like a boat in a heavy sea, and the dress-maker's eyes, distended with curiosity, sprang eagerly from face to face.

"I just thought I'd call in again," said Mr. Ramy, evidently somewhat disconcerted by the presence of Miss Mellins. "Just to see how the clock's behaving," he added with his hollow-cheeked smile.

"Oh, she's behaving beautiful," said Ann Eliza; "but we're real glad to see you all the same. Miss Mellins, let me make you acquainted with Mr. Ramy."

The dress-maker tossed back her head and dropped her lids in condescending recognition of the stranger's presence; and Mr. Ramy responded by an awkward bow. After the first moment of constraint a renewed sense of satisfaction filled the consciousness of the three women. The Bunner sisters were not sorry to let Miss Mellins see that they received an occasional evening visit, and Miss Mellins was clearly enchanted at the opportunity of pouring her latest tale into a new ear. As for Mr. Ramy, he adjusted himself to the situation with greater ease than might have been expected, and Evelina, who had been sorry that he should enter the room while the remains of supper still lingered on the table, blushed with pleasure at his good-humored offer to help her "glear away."

The table cleared, Ann Eliza suggested a game of cards; and it was after eleven o'clock when Mr. Ramy rose to take leave. His adieux were so much less abrupt than on the occasion of his first visit that Evelina was able to satisfy her sense of etiquette by escorting him, candle in hand, to the outer door; and as the two disappeared into the shop Miss Mellins playfully turned to Ann Eliza.

"Well, well, Miss Bunner," she murmured, jerking her chin in the direction of the retreating figures, "I'd no idea your sister was keeping company. On'y to think!"

Ann Eliza, roused from a state of dreamy beatitude, turned her timid eyes on the dress-maker.

"Oh, you're mistaken, Miss Mellins. We don't har'ly know Mr. Ramy."

Miss Mellins smiled incredulously. "You go 'long, Miss Bunner. I guess there'll be a wedding somewheres round here before spring, and I'll be real offended if I ain't asked to make the dress. I've always seen her in a gored satin with rooshings."

Ann Eliza made no answer. She had grown very pale, and her eyes lingered searchingly on Evelina as the younger sister re-entered the room. Evelina's cheeks were pink, and her blue eyes glittered; but it seemed to Ann Eliza that the coquettish tilt of her head regrettably emphasized the weakness of her receding chin. It was the first time that Ann Eliza had ever seen a flaw in her sister's beauty, and her involuntary criticism startled her like a secret disloyalty.

That night, after the light had been put out, the elder sister knelt longer than usual at her prayers. In the silence of the darkened room she was offering up certain dreams and aspirations whose brief blossoming had lent a transient freshness to her days.

She wondered now how she could ever have supposed that Mr. Ramy's visits had another cause than the one Miss Mellins suggested. Had not the sight of Evelina first inspired him with a sudden solicitude for the welfare of the clock? And what charms but Evelina's could have induced him to repeat his visit? Grief held up its torch to the frail fabric of Ann Eliza's illusions, and with a firm heart she watched them shrivel into ashes; then, rising from her knees full of the chill joy of renunciation, she laid a kiss on the crimping pins of the sleeping Evelina and crept under the bedspread at her side.

CHAPTER V

During the months that followed, Mr. Ramy visited the sisters with increasing frequency. It became his habit to call on them every Sunday evening, and occasionally during the week he would find an excuse for dropping in unannounced as they were settling down to their work beside the lamp. Ann Eliza noticed that Evelina now took the precaution of putting on her crimson bow every evening before supper, and that she had refurbished with a bit of carefully washed lace the black silk which they still called new because it had been bought a year after Ann Eliza's.

Mr. Ramy, as he grew more intimate, became less conversational, and after the sisters had blushingly accorded him the privilege of a pipe he began to permit himself long stretches of meditative silence that were not without charm to his hostesses. There was something at once fortifying and pacific in the sense of that tranquil male presence in an atmosphere which had so long quivered with little feminine doubts and distresses; and the sisters fell into the habit of saying to each other, in moments of uncertainty: "We'll ask Mr. Ramy when he comes," and of accepting his verdict, whatever it might be, with a fatalistic readiness that relieved them of all responsibility.

When Mr. Ramy drew the pipe from his mouth and became, in his turn, confidential, the acuteness of their sympathy grew almost painful to the sisters. With passionate participation they listened to the story of his early struggles in Germany, and of the long illness which had been the cause of his recent misfortunes. The name of the Mrs. Hochmuller (an old comrade's widow) who had nursed him through his fever was greeted with reverential sighs and an inward pang of envy whenever it recurred in his biographical monologues, and once when the sisters were alone Evelina called a responsive flush to Ann Eliza's brow by saying suddenly, without the mention of any name: "I wonder what she's like?"

One day toward spring Mr. Ramy, who had by this time become as much a part of their lives as the letter-carrier or the milkman, ventured the suggestion that the ladies should accompany him to an exhibition of stereopticon views which was to take place at Chickering Hall on the following evening.

After their first breathless "Oh!" of pleasure there was a silence of mutual consultation, which Ann Eliza at last broke by saying: "You better go with Mr. Ramy, Evelina. I guess we don't both want to leave the store at night."

Evelina, with such protests as politeness demanded, acquiesced in this opinion, and spent the next day in trimming a white chip bonnet with forget-me-nots of her own making. Ann Eliza brought out her mosaic brooch, a cashmere scarf of their mother's was taken from its linen cerements, and thus adorned Evelina blushingly departed with Mr. Ramy, while the elder sister sat down in her place at the pinking-machine.

It seemed to Ann Eliza that she was alone for hours, and she was surprised, when she heard Evelina tap on the door, to find that the clock marked only half-past ten.

"It must have gone wrong again," she reflected as she rose to let her sister in.

The evening had been brilliantly interesting, and several striking stereopticon views of Berlin had afforded Mr. Ramy the opportunity of enlarging on the marvels of his native city.

"He said he'd love to show it all to me!" Evelina declared as Ann Eliza conned her glowing face. "Did you ever hear anything so silly? I didn't know which way to look."

Ann Eliza received this confidence with a sympathetic murmur.

"My bonnet *is* becoming, isn't it?" Evelina went on irrelevantly, smiling at her reflection in the cracked glass above the chest of drawers.

"You're jest lovely," said Ann Eliza.

Spring was making itself unmistakably known to the distrustful New Yorker by an increased harshness of wind and prevalence of dust, when one day Evelina entered the back room at supper-time with a cluster of jonquils in her hand.

"I was just that foolish," she answered Ann Eliza's wondering glance, "I couldn't help buyin' 'em. I felt as if I must have something pretty to look at right away."

"Oh, sister," said Ann Eliza, in trembling sympathy. She felt that special indulgence must be conceded to those in Evelina's state since she had had her own fleeting vision of such mysterious longings as the words betrayed.

Evelina, meanwhile, had taken the bundle of dried grasses out of the broken china vase, and was putting the jonquils in their place with touches that lingered down their smooth stems and blade-like leaves.

"Ain't they pretty?" she kept repeating as she gathered the flowers into a starry circle. "Seems as if spring was really here, don't it?"

Ann Eliza remembered that it was Mr. Ramy's evening.

When he came, the Teutonic eye for anything that blooms made him turn at once to the jonquils.

"Ain't dey pretty?" he said. "Seems like as if de spring was really here."

"Don't it?" Evelina exclaimed, thrilled by the coincidence of their thought. "It's just what I was saying to my sister."

Ann Eliza got up suddenly and moved away; she remembered that she had not wound the clock the day before. Evelina was sitting at the table; the jonquils rose slenderly between herself and Mr. Ramy.

"Oh," she murmured with vague eyes, "how I'd love to get away somewheres into the country this very minute—somewheres where it was green and quiet. Seems as if I couldn't stand the city another day." But Ann Eliza noticed that she was looking at Mr. Ramy, and not at the flowers.

"I guess we might go to Cendral Park some Sunday," their visitor suggested. "Do you ever go there, Miss Evelina?"

"No, we don't very often; leastways we ain't been for a good while." She sparkled at the prospect. "It would be lovely, wouldn't it, Ann Eliza?"

"Why, yes," said the elder sister, coming back to her seat.

"Well, why don't we go next Sunday?" Mr. Ramy continued. "And we'll invite Miss Mellins too—that'll make a gosy little party."

That night when Evelina undressed she took a jonquil from the vase and pressed it with a certain ostentation between the leaves of her prayer-book. Ann Eliza, covertly observing her, felt that Evelina was not sorry to be observed, and that her own acute consciousness of the act was somehow regarded as magnifying its significance.

The following Sunday broke blue and warm. The Bunner sisters were habitual church-goers, but for once they left their prayer-books on the what-not, and ten o'clock found them, gloved and bonneted, awaiting Miss Mellins's knock. Miss Mellins presently appeared in a glitter of jet sequins and spangles, with a tale of having seen a strange man prowling under her windows till he was called off at dawn by a confederate's whistle; and shortly afterward came Mr. Ramy, his hair brushed with more than usual care, his broad hands encased in gloves of olive-green kid.

The little party set out for the nearest street-car, and a flutter of mingled gratification and embarrassment stirred Ann Eliza's bosom when it was found that Mr. Ramy intended to pay their fares. Nor did he fail to live up to this opening liberality; for after guiding them through the Mall and the Ramble he led the way to a rustic restaurant where, also at his expense, they fared idyllically on milk and lemon-pie.

After this they resumed their walk, strolling on with the slowness of unaccustomed holiday-makers from one path to another—through budding shrubberies, past grass-banks sprinkled with lilac crocuses, and under rocks on which the forsythia lay like sudden sunshine. Everything about her seemed new and miraculously lovely to Ann Eliza; but she kept her feelings to herself, leaving it to Evelina to exclaim at the hepaticas under the shady ledges, and to Miss Mellins, less interested in the vegetable than in the human world, to remark significantly on the probable history of the persons they met. All the alleys were thronged with promenaders and obstructed by perambulators; and Miss Mellins's running commentary threw a glare of lurid possibilities over the placid family groups and their romping progeny.

Ann Eliza was in no mood for such interpretations of life; but, knowing that Miss Mellins had been invited for the sole purpose of keeping her company she continued to cling to the dress-maker's side, letting Mr. Ramy lead the way with Evelina. Miss Mellins, stimulated by the excitement of the occasion, grew more and more discursive, and her ceaseless talk, and the kaleidoscopic whirl of the crowd, were unspeakably bewildering to Ann Eliza. Her feet, accustomed to the slippered ease of the shop, ached with the unfamiliar effort of walking, and her ears with the din of the dress-maker's anecdotes; but every nerve in her was aware of Evelina's enjoyment, and she was determined that no weariness of hers should curtail it. Yet even her heroism shrank from the significant glances which Miss Mellins presently began to cast at the couple in front of them: Ann Eliza could bear to connive at Evelina's bliss, but not to acknowledge it to others.

At length Evelina's feet also failed her, and she turned to suggest that they ought to be going home. Her flushed face had grown pale with fatigue, but her eyes were radiant.

The return lived in Ann Eliza's memory with the persistence of an evil dream. The horse-cars were packed with the returning throng, and they had to let a dozen go by before they could push their way into one that was already crowded. Ann Eliza had never before felt so tired. Even Miss Mellins's flow of narrative ran dry, and they sat silent, wedged between a negro woman and a pock-marked man with a bandaged head, while the car rumbled slowly down a squalid avenue to their corner. Evelina and Mr. Ramy sat together in the forward part of the car, and Ann Eliza could catch only an occasional glimpse of the forget-me-not bonnet and the clock-maker's shiny coat-collar; but when the little party got out at their corner the crowd swept them together again, and they walked back in the effortless silence of tired children to the Bunner sisters' basement. As Miss Mellins and Mr. Ramy turned to go their various ways Evelina mustered a last display of smiles; but Ann Eliza crossed the threshold in silence, feeling the stillness of the little shop reach out to her like consoling arms.

That night she could not sleep; but as she lay cold and rigid at her sister's side, she suddenly felt the pressure of Evelina's arms, and heard her whisper: "Oh, Ann Eliza, warn't it heavenly?"

CHAPTER VI

For four days after their Sunday in the Park the Bunner sisters had no news of Mr. Ramy. At first neither one betrayed her disappointment and anxiety to the other; but on the fifth morning Evelina, always the first to yield to her feelings, said, as she turned from her untasted tea: "I thought you'd oughter take that money out by now, Ann Eliza."

Ann Eliza understood and reddened. The winter had been a fairly prosperous one for the sisters, and their slowly accumulated savings had now reached the handsome sum of two hundred dollars; but the satisfaction they might have felt in this unwonted opulence had been clouded by a suggestion of Miss Mellins's that there were dark rumours concerning the savings bank in which their funds were deposited. They knew Miss Mellins was given to vain alarms; but her words, by the sheer force of repetition, had so shaken Ann Eliza's peace that after long hours of midnight counsel the sisters had decided to advise with Mr. Ramy; and on Ann Eliza, as the head of the house, this duty had devolved. Mr. Ramy, when consulted, had not only confirmed the dress-maker's report, but had offered to find some safe investment which should give the sisters a higher rate of interest than the suspected savings bank; and Ann Eliza knew that Evelina alluded to the suggested transfer.

"Why, yes, to be sure," she agreed. "Mr. Ramy said if he was us he wouldn't want to leave his money there any longer'n he could help."

"It was over a week ago he said it," Evelina reminded her.

"I know; but he told me to wait till he'd found out for sure about that other investment; and we ain't seen him since then."

Ann Eliza's words released their secret fear. "I wonder what's happened to him," Evelina said. "You don't suppose he could be sick?"

"I was wondering too," Ann Eliza rejoined; and the sisters looked down at their plates.

"I should think you'd oughter do something about that money pretty soon," Evelina began again.

"Well, I know I'd oughter. What would you do if you was me?"

"If I was *you*," said her sister, with perceptible emphasis and a rising blush, "I'd go right round and see if Mr. Ramy was sick. *You* could."

The words pierced Ann Eliza like a blade. "Yes, that's so," she said.

"It would only seem friendly, if he really *is* sick. If I was you I'd go to-day," Evelina continued; and after dinner Ann Eliza went.

On the way she had to leave a parcel at the dyer's, and having performed that errand she turned toward Mr. Ramy's shop. Never before had she felt so old, so hopeless and humble. She knew she was bound on a love-errand of Evelina's, and the knowledge seemed to dry the last drop of young blood in her veins. It took from her, too, all her faded virginal shyness; and with a brisk composure she turned the handle of the clock-maker's door.

But as she entered her heart began to tremble, for she saw Mr. Ramy, his face hidden in his hands, sitting behind the counter in an attitude of strange dejection. At the click of the latch he looked up slowly, fixing a lustreless stare on Ann Eliza. For a moment she thought he did not know her.

"Oh, you're sick!" she exclaimed; and the sound of her voice seemed to recall his wandering senses.

"Why, if it ain't Miss Bunner!" he said, in a low thick tone; but he made no attempt to move, and she noticed that his face was the colour of yellow ashes.

"You *are* sick," she persisted, emboldened by his evident need of help. "Mr. Ramy, it was real unfriendly of you not to let us know."

He continued to look at her with dull eyes. "I ain't been sick," he said. "Leastways not very: only one of my old turns." He spoke in a slow laboured way, as if he had difficulty in getting his words together.

"Rheumatism?" she ventured, seeing how unwillingly he seemed to move.

"Well—somethin' like, maybe. I couldn't hardly put a name to it."

"If it *was* anything like rheumatism, my grandmother used to make a tea—" Ann Eliza began: she had forgotten, in the warmth of the moment, that she had only come as Evelina's messenger.

At the mention of tea an expression of uncontrollable repugnance passed over Mr. Ramy's face. "Oh, I guess I'm getting on all right. I've just got a headache to-day."

Ann Eliza's courage dropped at the note of refusal in his voice.

"I'm sorry," she said gently. "My sister and me'd have been glad to do anything we could for you."

"Thank you kindly," said Mr. Ramy wearily; then, as she turned to the door, he added with an effort: "Maybe I'll step round to-morrow."

"We'll be real glad," Ann Eliza repeated. Her eyes were fixed on a dusty bronze clock in the window. She was unaware of looking at it at the time, but long afterward she remembered that it represented a Newfoundland dog with his paw on an open book.

When she reached home there was a purchaser in the shop, turning over hooks and eyes under Evelina's absent-minded supervision. Ann Eliza passed hastily into the back room, but in an instant she heard her sister at her side.

"Quick! I told her I was goin' to look for some smaller hooks—how is he?" Evelina gasped.

"He ain't been very well," said Ann Eliza slowly, her eyes on Evelina's eager face; "but he says he'll be sure to be round to-morrow night."

"He will? Are you telling me the truth?"

"Why, Evelina Bunner!"

"Oh, I don't care!" cried the younger recklessly, rushing back into the shop.

Ann Eliza stood burning with the shame of Evelina's self-exposure. She was shocked that, even to her, Evelina should lay bare the nakedness of her emotion; and she tried to turn her thoughts from it as though its recollection made her a sharer in her sister's debasement.

The next evening, Mr. Ramy reappeared, still somewhat sallow and red-lidded, but otherwise his usual self. Ann Eliza consulted him about the investment he had recommended, and after it had been settled that he should attend to the matter for her he took up the illustrated volume of Longfellow—for, as the sisters had learned, his culture soared beyond the newspapers—and read aloud, with a fine confusion of consonants, the poem on "Maidenhood." Evelina lowered her lids while he read. It was a very beautiful evening, and Ann Eliza thought afterward how different life might have been with a companion who read poetry like Mr. Ramy.

CHAPTER VII

During the ensuing weeks Mr. Ramy, though his visits were as frequent as ever, did not seem to regain his usual spirits. He complained frequently of headache, but rejected Ann Eliza's tentatively proffered remedies, and seemed to shrink from any prolonged investigation of his symptoms. July had come, with a sudden ardour of heat, and one evening, as the three sat together by the open window in the back room, Evelina said: "I dunno what I wouldn't give, a night like this, for a breath of real country air."

"So would I," said Mr. Ramy, knocking the ashes from his pipe. "I'd like to be setting in an arbour dis very minute."

"Oh, wouldn't it be lovely?"

"I always think it's real cool here—we'd be heaps hotter up where Miss Mellins is," said Ann Eliza.

"Oh, I daresay—but we'd be heaps cooler somewhere else," her sister snapped: she was not infrequently exasperated by Ann Eliza's furtive attempts to mollify Providence.

A few days later Mr. Ramy appeared with a suggestion which enchanted Evelina. He had gone the day before to see his friend, Mrs. Hochmuller, who lived in the outskirts of Hoboken, and Mrs. Hochmuller had proposed that on the following Sunday he should bring the Bunner sisters to spend the day with her.

"She's got a real garden, you know," Mr. Ramy explained, "wid trees and a real summer-house to set in; and hens and chickens too. And it's an elegant sail over on de ferry-boat."

The proposal drew no response from Ann Eliza. She was still oppressed by the recollection of her interminable Sunday in the Park; but, obedient to Evelina's imperious glance, she finally faltered out an acceptance.

The Sunday was a very hot one, and once on the ferry-boat Ann Eliza revived at the touch of the salt breeze, and the spectacle of the crowded waters; but when they reached the other shore, and stepped out on the dirty wharf, she began to ache with anticipated weariness. They got into a street-car, and were jolted from one mean street to another, till at length Mr. Ramy pulled the conductor's sleeve and they got out again; then they stood in the blazing sun, near the door of a crowded beer-saloon, waiting for another car to come; and that carried them out to a thinly settled district, past vacant lots and narrow brick houses standing in unsupported solitude, till they finally reached an almost rural region of scattered cottages and low wooden buildings that looked like village "stores." Here the car finally stopped of its own accord, and they walked along a rutty road, past a stone-cutter's yard with a high fence tapestried with theatrical advertisements, to a little red house with green blinds and a garden paling. Really, Mr. Ramy had not deceived them. Clumps of dielytra and day-lilies bloomed behind the paling, and a crooked elm hung romantically over the gable of the house.

At the gate Mrs. Hochmuller, a broad woman in brick-brown merino, met them with nods and smiles, while her daughter Linda, a flaxen-haired girl with mottled red cheeks and a sidelong stare, hovered inquisitively behind her. Mrs. Hochmuller, leading the way into the house, conducted the Bunner sisters the way to her bedroom. Here they were invited to spread out on a mountainous white featherbed the cashmere mantles under which the solemnity of the occasion had compelled them to swelter, and when they had given their black silks the necessary twitch of readjustment, and Evelina had fluffed out her hair before a looking-glass framed in pink-shell work, their hostess led them to a stuffy parlour smelling of gingerbread. After another ceremonial pause, broken by polite enquiries and shy ejaculations, they were shown into the kitchen, where the table was already spread with strange-looking spice-cakes and stewed fruits, and where they presently found themselves seated between Mrs. Hochmuller and Mr. Ramy, while the staring Linda bumped back and forth from the stove with steaming dishes.

To Ann Eliza the dinner seemed endless, and the rich fare strangely unappetizing. She was abashed by the easy intimacy of her hostess's voice and eye. With Mr. Ramy Mrs. Hochmuller was almost flippantly familiar, and it was only when Ann Eliza pictured her generous form bent above his sick-bed that she could forgive her for tersely addressing him as "Ramy." During one of the pauses of the meal Mrs. Hochmuller laid her knife and fork against the edges of her plate, and, fixing her eyes on the clock-maker's face, said accusingly: "You hat one of dem turns again, Ramy."

"I dunno as I had," he returned evasively.

Evelina glanced from one to the other. "Mr. Ramy *has* been sick," she said at length, as though to show that she also was in a position to speak with authority. "He's complained very frequently of headaches."

"Ho!—I know him," said Mrs. Hochmuller with a laugh, her eyes still on the clock-maker. "Ain't you ashamed of yourself, Ramy?"

Mr. Ramy, who was looking at his plate, said suddenly one word which the sisters could not understand; it sounded to Ann Eliza like "Shwike."

Mrs. Hochmuller laughed again. "My, my," she said, "wouldn't you think he'd be ashamed to go and be sick and never dell me, me that nursed him troo dat awful fever?"

"Yes, I *should*," said Evelina, with a spirited glance at Ramy; but he was looking at the sausages that Linda had just put on the table.

When dinner was over Mrs. Hochmuller invited her guests to step out of the kitchen-door, and they found themselves in a green enclosure, half garden, half orchard. Grey hens followed by golden broods clucked under the twisted apple-boughs, a cat dozed on the edge of an old well, and from tree to tree ran the network of clothes-line that denoted Mrs. Hochmuller's calling. Beyond the apple trees stood a yellow summer-house festooned with scarlet runners; and below it, on the farther side of a rough fence, the land dipped down, holding a bit of woodland in its hollow. It was all strangely sweet and still on that hot Sunday afternoon, and as she moved across the grass under the apple-boughs Ann Eliza thought of quiet afternoons in church, and of the hymns her mother had sung to her when she was a baby.

Evelina was more restless. She wandered from the well to the summer-house and back, she tossed crumbs to the chickens and disturbed the cat with arch caresses; and at last she expressed a desire to go down into the wood.

"I guess you got to go round by the road, then," said Mrs. Hochmuller. "My Linda she goes troo a hole in de fence, but I guess you'd tear your dress if you was to dry."

"I'll help you," said Mr. Ramy; and guided by Linda the pair walked along the fence till they reached a narrow gap in its boards. Through this they disappeared, watched curiously in their descent by the grinning Linda, while Mrs. Hochmuller and Ann Eliza were left alone in the summer-house.

Mrs. Hochmuller looked at her guest with a confidential smile. "I guess dey'll be gone quite a while," she remarked, jerking her double chin toward the gap in the fence. "Folks like dat don't never remember about de dime." And she drew out her knitting.

Ann Eliza could think of nothing to say.

"Your sister she thinks a great lot of him, don't she?" her hostess continued.

Ann Eliza's cheeks grew hot. "Ain't you a teeny bit lonesome away out here sometimes?" she asked. "I should think you'd be scared nights, all alone with your daughter."

"Oh, no, I ain't," said Mrs. Hochmuller. "You see I take in washing—dat's my business—and it's a lot cheaper doing it out here dan in de city: where'd I get a drying-ground like dis in Hobucken? And den it's safer for Linda too; it geeps her outer de streets."

"Oh," said Ann Eliza, shrinking. She began to feel a distinct aversion for her hostess, and her eyes turned with involuntary annoyance to the square-backed form of Linda, still inquisitively suspended on the fence. It seemed to Ann Eliza that Evelina and her companion would never return from the wood; but they came at length, Mr. Ramy's brow pearled with perspiration, Evelina pink and conscious, a drooping bunch of ferns in her hand; and it was clear that, to her at least, the moments had been winged.

"D'you suppose they'll revive?" she asked, holding up the ferns; but Ann Eliza, rising at her approach, said stiffly: "We'd better be getting home, Evelina."

"Mercy me! Ain't you going to take your coffee first?" Mrs. Hochmuller protested; and Ann Eliza found to her dismay that another long gastronomic ceremony must intervene before politeness permitted them to leave. At length, however, they found themselves again on the ferry-boat. Water and sky were grey, with a dividing gleam of sunset that sent sleek opal waves in the boat's wake. The wind had a cool tarry breath, as though it had travelled over miles of shipping, and the hiss of the water about the paddles was as delicious as though it had been splashed into their tired faces.

Ann Eliza sat apart, looking away from the others. She had made up her mind that Mr. Ramy had proposed to Evelina in the wood, and she was silently preparing herself to receive her sister's confidence that evening.

But Evelina was apparently in no mood for confidences. When they reached home she put her faded ferns in water, and after supper, when she had laid aside her silk dress and the forget-me-not bonnet, she remained silently seated in her rocking-chair near the open window. It was long since Ann Eliza had seen her in so uncommunicative a mood.

The following Saturday Ann Eliza was sitting alone in the shop when the door opened and Mr. Ramy entered. He had never before called at that hour, and she wondered a little anxiously what had brought him.

"Has anything happened?" she asked, pushing aside the basketful of buttons she had been sorting.

"Not's I know of," said Mr. Ramy tranquilly. "But I always close up the store at two o'clock Saturdays at this season, so I thought I might as well call round and see you."

"I'm real glad, I'm sure," said Ann Eliza; "but Evelina's out."

"I know dat," Mr. Ramy answered. "I met her round de corner. She told me she got to go to dat new dyer's up in Forty-eighth Street. She won't be back for a couple of hours, har'ly, will she?"

Ann Eliza looked at him with rising bewilderment. "No, I guess not," she answered; her instinctive hospitality prompting her to add: "Won't you set down jest the same?"

Mr. Ramy sat down on the stool beside the counter, and Ann Eliza returned to her place behind it.

"I can't leave the store," she explained.

"Well, I guess we're very well here." Ann Eliza had become suddenly aware that Mr. Ramy was looking at her with unusual intentness. Involuntarily her hand strayed to the thin streaks of hair on her temples, and thence descended to straighten the brooch beneath her collar.

"You're looking very well to-day, Miss Bunner," said Mr. Ramy, following her gesture with a smile.

"Oh," said Ann Eliza nervously. "I'm always well in health," she added.

"I guess you're healthier than your sister, even if you are less sizeable."

"Oh, I don't know. Evelina's a mite nervous sometimes, but she ain't a bit sickly."

"She eats heartier than you do; but that don't mean nothing," said Mr. Ramy.

Ann Eliza was silent. She could not follow the trend of his thought, and she did not care to commit herself farther about Evelina before she had ascertained if Mr. Ramy considered nervousness interesting or the reverse.

But Mr. Ramy spared her all farther indecision.

"Well, Miss Bunner," he said, drawing his stool closer to the counter, "I guess I might as well tell you fust as last what I come here for to-day. I want to get married."

Ann Eliza, in many a prayerful midnight hour, had sought to strengthen herself for the hearing of this avowal, but now that it had come she felt pitifully frightened and unprepared. Mr. Ramy was leaning with both elbows on the counter, and she noticed that his nails were clean and that he had brushed his hat; yet even these signs had not prepared her!

At last she heard herself say, with a dry throat in which her heart was hammering: "Mercy me, Mr. Ramy!"

"I want to get married," he repeated. "I'm too lonesome. It ain't good for a man to live all alone, and eat noding but cold meat every day."

"No," said Ann Eliza softly.

"And the dust fairly beats me."

"Oh, the dust—I know!"

Mr. Ramy stretched one of his blunt-fingered hands toward her. "I wisht you'd take me."

Still Ann Eliza did not understand. She rose hesitatingly from her seat, pushing aside the basket of buttons which lay between them; then she perceived that Mr. Ramy was trying to take her hand, and as their fingers met a flood of joy swept over her. Never afterward, though every other word of their interview was stamped on her memory beyond all possible forgetting, could she recall what he said while their hands touched; she only knew that she seemed to be floating on a summer sea, and that all its waves were in her ears.

"Me—me?" she gasped.

"I guess so," said her suitor placidly. "You suit me right down to the ground, Miss Bunner. Dat's the truth."

A woman passing along the street paused to look at the shop-window, and Ann Eliza half hoped she would come in; but after a desultory inspection she went on.

"Maybe you don't fancy me?" Mr. Ramy suggested, discountenanced by Ann Eliza's silence.

A word of assent was on her tongue, but her lips refused it. She must find some other way of telling him.

"I don't say that."

"Well, I always kinder thought we was suited to one another," Mr. Ramy continued, eased of his momentary doubt. "I always liked de quiet style—no fuss and airs, and not afraid of work." He spoke as though dispassionately cataloguing her charms.

Ann Eliza felt that she must make an end. "But, Mr. Ramy, you don't understand. I've never thought of marrying."

Mr. Ramy looked at her in surprise. "Why not?"

"Well, I don't know, har'ly." She moistened her twitching lips. "The fact is, I ain't as active as I look. Maybe I couldn't stand the care. I ain't as spry as Evelina—nor as young," she added, with a last great effort.

"But you do most of de work here, anyways," said her suitor doubtfully.

"Oh, well, that's because Evelina's busy outside; and where there's only two women the work don't amount to much. Besides, I'm the oldest; I have to look after things," she hastened on, half pained that her simple ruse should so readily deceive him.

"Well, I guess you're active enough for me," he persisted. His calm determination began to frighten her; she trembled lest her own should be less staunch.

"No, no," she repeated, feeling the tears on her lashes. "I couldn't, Mr. Ramy, I couldn't marry. I'm so surprised. I always thought it was Evelina—always. And so did everybody else. She's so bright and pretty—it seemed so natural."

"Well, you was all mistaken," said Mr. Ramy obstinately.

"I'm so sorry."

He rose, pushing back his chair.

"You'd better think it over," he said, in the large tone of a man who feels he may safely wait.

"Oh, no, no. It ain't any sorter use, Mr. Ramy. I don't never mean to marry. I get tired so easily—I'd be afraid of the work. And I have such awful headaches." She paused, racking her brain for more convincing infirmities.

"Headaches, do you?" said Mr. Ramy, turning back.

"My, yes, awful ones, that I have to give right up to. Evelina has to do everything when I have one of them headaches. She has to bring me my tea in the mornings."

"Well, I'm sorry to hear it," said Mr. Ramy.

"Thank you kindly all the same," Ann Eliza murmured. "And please don't—don't—" She stopped suddenly, looking at him through her tears.

"Oh, that's all right," he answered. "Don't you fret, Miss Gunner. Folks have got to suit themselves." She thought his tone had grown more resigned since she had spoken of her headaches.

For some moments he stood looking at her with a hesitating eye, as though uncertain how to end their conversation; and at length she found courage to say (in the words of a novel she had once read): "I don't want this should make any difference between us."

"Oh, my, no," said Mr. Ramy, absently picking up his hat.

"You'll come in just the same?" she continued, nerving herself to the effort. "We'd miss you awfully if you didn't. Evelina, she—" She paused, torn between her desire to turn his thoughts to Evelina, and the dread of prematurely disclosing her sister's secret.

"Don't Miss Evelina have no headaches?" Mr. Ramy suddenly asked.

"My, no, never—well, not to speak of, anyway. She ain't had one for ages, and when Evelina *is* sick she won't never give in to it," Ann Eliza declared, making some hurried adjustments with her conscience.

"I wouldn't have thought that," said Mr. Ramy.

"I guess you don't know us as well as you thought you did."

"Well, no, that's so; maybe I don't. I'll wish you good day, Miss Bunner"; and Mr. Ramy moved toward the door.

"Good day, Mr. Ramy," Ann Eliza answered.

She felt unutterably thankful to be alone. She knew the crucial moment of her life had passed, and she was glad that she had not fallen below her own ideals. It had been a wonderful experience; and in spite of the tears on her cheeks she was not sorry to have known it. Two facts, however, took the edge from its perfection: that it had happened in the shop, and that she had not had on her black silk.

She passed the next hour in a state of dreamy ecstasy. Something had entered into her life of which no subsequent empoverishment could rob it: she glowed with the same rich sense of possessorship that once, as a little girl, she had felt when her mother had given her a gold locket and she had sat up in bed in the dark to draw it from its hiding-place beneath her night-gown.

At length a dread of Evelina's return began to mingle with these musings. How could she meet her younger sister's eye without betraying what had happened? She felt as though a visible glory lay on her, and she was glad that dusk had fallen when Evelina entered. But her fears were superfluous. Evelina, always self-absorbed, had of late lost all interest in the simple happenings of the shop, and Ann Eliza, with mingled mortification and relief, perceived that she was in no danger of being cross-questioned as to the events of the afternoon. She was glad of this; yet there was a touch of humiliation in finding that the portentous secret in her bosom did not visibly shine forth. It struck her as dull, and even slightly absurd, of Evelina not to know at last that they were equals.

PART-II

CHAPTER VIII

Mr. Ramy, after a decent interval, returned to the shop; and Ann Eliza, when they met, was unable to detect whether the emotions which seethed under her black alpaca found an echo in his bosom. Outwardly he made no sign. He lit his pipe as placidly as ever and seemed to relapse without effort into the unruffled intimacy of old. Yet to Ann Eliza's initiated eye a change became gradually perceptible. She saw that he was beginning to look at her sister as he had looked at her on that momentous afternoon: she even discerned a secret significance in the turn of his talk with Evelina. Once he asked her abruptly if she should like to travel, and Ann Eliza saw that the flush on Evelina's cheek was reflected from the same fire which had scorched her own.

So they drifted on through the sultry weeks of July. At that season the business of the little shop almost ceased, and one Saturday morning Mr. Ramy proposed that the sisters should lock up early and go with him for a sail down the bay in one of the Coney Island boats.

Ann Eliza saw the light in Evelina's eye and her resolve was instantly taken.

"I guess I won't go, thank you kindly; but I'm sure my sister will be happy to."

She was pained by the perfunctory phrase with which Evelina urged her to accompany them; and still more by Mr. Ramy's silence.

"No, I guess I won't go," she repeated, rather in answer to herself than to them. "It's dreadfully hot and I've got a kinder headache."

"Oh, well, I wouldn't then," said her sister hurriedly. "You'd better jest set here quietly and rest."

"Yes, I'll rest," Ann Eliza assented.

At two o'clock Mr. Ramy returned, and a moment later he and Evelina left the shop. Evelina had made herself another new bonnet for the occasion, a bonnet, Ann Eliza thought, almost too youthful in shape and colour. It was the first time it had ever occurred to her to criticize Evelina's taste, and she was frightened at the insidious change in her attitude toward her sister.

When Ann Eliza, in later days, looked back on that afternoon she felt that there had been something prophetic in the quality of its solitude; it seemed to distill the triple essence of loneliness in which all her after-life was to be lived. No purchasers came; not a hand fell on the door-latch; and the tick of the clock in the back room ironically emphasized the passing of the empty hours.

Evelina returned late and alone. Ann Eliza felt the coming crisis in the sound of her footstep, which wavered along as if not knowing on what it trod. The elder sister's affection had so passionately projected itself into her junior's fate that at such moments she seemed to be living two lives, her own and Evelina's; and her private longings shrank into silence at the sight of the other's hungry bliss. But it was evident that Evelina, never acutely alive to the emotional atmosphere about her, had no idea that her secret was suspected; and with an assumption of unconcern that would have made Ann Eliza smile if the pang had been less piercing, the younger sister prepared to confess herself.

"What are you so busy about?" she said impatiently, as Ann Eliza, beneath the gas-jet, fumbled for the matches. "Ain't you even got time to ask me if I'd had a pleasant day?"

Ann Eliza turned with a quiet smile. "I guess I don't have to. Seems to me it's pretty plain you have."

"Well, I don't know. I don't know *how* I feel—it's all so queer. I almost think I'd like to scream."

"I guess you're tired."

"No, I ain't. It's not that. But it all happened so suddenly, and the boat was so crowded I thought everybody'd hear what he was saying.—Ann Eliza," she broke out, "why on earth don't you ask me what I'm talking about?"

Ann Eliza, with a last effort of heroism, feigned a fond incomprehension.

"What *are* you?"

"Why, I'm engaged to be married—so there! Now it's out! And it happened right on the boat; only to think of it! Of course I wasn't exactly surprised—I've known right along he was going to sooner or later—on'y somehow I didn't think of its happening to-day. I thought he'd never get up his courage. He said he was so 'fraid I'd say no—that's what kep' him so long from asking me. Well, I ain't said yes *yet*—leastways I told him I'd have to think it over; but I guess he knows. Oh, Ann Eliza, I'm so happy!" She hid the blinding brightness of her face.

Ann Eliza, just then, would only let herself feel that she was glad. She drew down Evelina's hands and kissed her, and they held each other. When Evelina regained her voice she had a tale to tell which carried their vigil far into the night. Not a syllable, not a glance or gesture of Ramy's, was the elder sister spared; and with unconscious irony she found herself comparing the details of his proposal to her with those which Evelina was imparting with merciless prolixity.

The next few days were taken up with the embarrassed adjustment of their new relation to Mr. Ramy and to each other. Ann Eliza's ardour carried her to new heights of self-effacement, and she invented late duties in the shop in order to leave Evelina and her suitor longer alone in the back room. Later on, when she tried to remember the details of those first days, few came back to her: she knew only that she got up each morning with the sense of having to push the leaden hours up the same long steep of pain.

Mr. Ramy came daily now. Every evening he and his betrothed went out for a stroll around the Square, and when Evelina came in her cheeks were always pink. "He's kissed her under that tree at the corner, away from the lamp-post," Ann Eliza said to herself, with sudden insight into unconjectured things. On Sundays they usually went for the whole afternoon to the Central Park, and Ann Eliza, from her seat in the mortal hush of the back room, followed step by step their long slow beatific walk.

There had been, as yet, no allusion to their marriage, except that Evelina had once told her sister that Mr. Ramy wished them to invite Mrs. Hochmuller and Linda to the wedding. The mention of the laundress raised a half-forgotten fear in Ann Eliza, and she said in a tone of tentative appeal: "I guess if I was you I wouldn't want to be very great friends with Mrs. Hochmuller."

Evelina glanced at her compassionately. "I guess if you was me you'd want to do everything you could to please the man you loved. It's lucky," she added with glacial irony, "that I'm not too grand for Herman's friends."

"Oh," Ann Eliza protested, "that ain't what I mean—and you know it ain't. Only somehow the day we saw her I didn't think she seemed like the kinder person you'd want for a friend."

"I guess a married woman's the best judge of such matters," Evelina replied, as though she already walked in the light of her future state.

Ann Eliza, after that, kept her own counsel. She saw that Evelina wanted her sympathy as little as her admonitions, and that already she counted for nothing in her sister's scheme of life. To Ann Eliza's idolatrous acceptance of the cruelties of fate this exclusion seemed both natural and just; but it caused her the most lively pain. She could not divest her love for Evelina of its passionate motherliness; no breath of reason could lower it to the cool temperature of sisterly affection.

She was then passing, as she thought, through the novitiate of her pain; preparing, in a hundred experimental ways, for the solitude awaiting her when Evelina left. It was true that it would be a tempered loneliness. They would not be far apart. Evelina would "run in" daily from the clock-maker's; they would doubtless take supper with her on Sundays. But already Ann Eliza guessed with what growing perfunctoriness her sister would fulfill these obligations; she even foresaw the day when, to get news of Evelina, she should have to lock the shop at nightfall and go herself to Mr. Ramy's door. But on that contingency she would not dwell. "They can come to me when they want to—they'll always find me here," she simply said to herself.

One evening Evelina came in flushed and agitated from her stroll around the Square. Ann Eliza saw at once that something had happened; but the new habit of reticence checked her question.

She had not long to wait. "Oh, Ann Eliza, on'y to think what he says—" (the pronoun stood exclusively for Mr. Ramy). "I declare I'm so upset I thought the people in the Square would notice me. Don't I look queer? He wants to get married right off—this very next week."

"Next week?"

"Yes. So's we can move out to St. Louis right away."

"Him and you—move out to St. Louis?"

"Well, I don't know as it would be natural for him to want to go out there without me," Evelina simpered. "But it's all so sudden I don't know what to think. He only got the letter this morning. *Do* I look queer, Ann Eliza?" Her eye was roving for the mirror.

"No, you don't," said Ann Eliza almost harshly.

"Well, it's a mercy," Evelina pursued with a tinge of disappointment. "It's a regular miracle I didn't faint right out there in the Square. Herman's so thoughtless—he just put the letter into my hand without a word. It's from a big firm out there—the Tiff'ny of St. Louis, he says it is—offering him a place in their clock-department. Seems they heard of him through a German friend of his that's settled out there. It's a splendid opening, and if he gives satisfaction they'll raise him at the end of the year."

She paused, flushed with the importance of the situation, which seemed to lift her once for all above the dull level of her former life.

"Then you'll have to go?" came at last from Ann Eliza.

Evelina stared. "You wouldn't have me interfere with his prospects, would you?"

"No—no. I on'y meant—has it got to be so soon?"

"Right away, I tell you—next week. Ain't it awful?" blushed the bride.

Well, this was what happened to mothers. They bore it, Ann Eliza mused; so why not she? Ah, but they had their own chance first; she had had no chance at all. And now this life which she had made her own was going from her forever; had gone, already, in the inner and deeper sense, and was soon to vanish in even its outward nearness, its surface-communion of voice and eye. At that moment even the thought of Evelina's happiness refused her its consolatory ray; or its light, if she saw it, was too remote to warm her. The thirst for a personal and inalienable tie, for pangs and problems of her own, was parching Ann Eliza's soul: it seemed to her that she could never again gather strength to look her loneliness in the face.

The trivial obligations of the moment came to her aid. Nursed in idleness her grief would have mastered her; but the needs of the shop and the back room, and the preparations for Evelina's marriage, kept the tyrant under.

Miss Mellins, true to her anticipations, had been called on to aid in the making of the wedding dress, and she and Ann Eliza were bending one evening over the breadths of pearl-grey cashmere which in spite of the dress-maker's prophetic vision of gored satin, had been judged most suitable, when Evelina came into the room alone.

Ann Eliza had already had occasion to notice that it was a bad sign when Mr. Ramy left his affianced at the door. It generally meant that Evelina had something disturbing to communicate, and Ann Eliza's first glance told her that this time the news was grave.

Miss Mellins, who sat with her back to the door and her head bent over her sewing, started as Evelina came around to the opposite side of the table.

"Mercy, Miss Evelina! I declare I thought you was a ghost, the way you crep' in. I had a customer once up in Forty-ninth Street—a lovely young woman with a thirty-six bust and a waist you could ha' put into her wedding ring—and her husband, he crep' up behind her that way jest for a joke, and frightened her into a fit, and when she come to she was a raving maniac, and had to be taken to Bloomingdale with two doctors and a nurse to hold her in the carriage, and a lovely baby on'y six weeks old—and there she is to this day, poor creature."

"I didn't mean to startle you," said Evelina.

She sat down on the nearest chair, and as the lamp-light fell on her face Ann Eliza saw that she had been crying.

"You do look dead-beat," Miss Mellins resumed, after a pause of soul-probing scrutiny. "I guess Mr. Ramy lugs you round that Square too often. You'll walk your legs off if you ain't careful. Men don't never consider—they're all alike. Why, I had a cousin once that was engaged to a book-agent—"

"Maybe we'd better put away the work for to-night, Miss Mellins," Ann Eliza interposed. "I guess what Evelina wants is a good night's rest."

"That's so," assented the dress-maker. "Have you got the back breadths run together, Miss Bunner? Here's the sleeves. I'll pin 'em together." She drew a cluster of pins from her mouth, in which she seemed to secrete them as squirrels stow away nuts. "There," she said, rolling up her work, "you go right away to bed, Miss Evelina, and we'll set up a little later to-morrow night. I guess you're a mite nervous, ain't you? I know when my turn comes I'll be scared to death."

With this arch forecast she withdrew, and Ann Eliza, returning to the back room, found Evelina still listlessly seated by the table. True to her new policy of silence, the elder sister set about folding up the bridal dress; but suddenly Evelina said in a harsh unnatural voice: "There ain't any use in going on with that."

The folds slipped from Ann Eliza's hands.

"Evelina Bunner—what you mean?"

"Jest what I say. It's put off."

"Put off—what's put off?"

"Our getting married. He can't take me to St. Louis. He ain't got money enough." She brought the words out in the monotonous tone of a child reciting a lesson.

Ann Eliza picked up another breadth of cashmere and began to smooth it out. "I don't understand," she said at length.

"Well, it's plain enough. The journey's fearfully expensive, and we've got to have something left to start with when we get out there. We've counted up, and he ain't got the money to do it—that's all."

"But I thought he was going right into a splendid place."

"So he is; but the salary's pretty low the first year, and board's very high in St. Louis. He's jest got another letter from his German friend, and he's been figuring it out, and he's afraid to chance it. He'll have to go alone."

"But there's your money—have you forgotten that? The hundred dollars in the bank."

Evelina made an impatient movement. "Of course I ain't forgotten it. On'y it ain't enough. It would all have to go into buying furniture, and if he was took sick and lost his place again we wouldn't have a cent left. He says he's got to lay by another hundred dollars before he'll be willing to take me out there."

For a while Ann Eliza pondered this surprising statement; then she ventured: "Seems to me he might have thought of it before."

In an instant Evelina was aflame. "I guess he knows what's right as well as you or me. I'd sooner die than be a burden to him."

Ann Eliza made no answer. The clutch of an unformulated doubt had checked the words on her lips. She had meant, on the day of her sister's marriage, to give Evelina the other half of their common savings; but something warned her not to say so now.

The sisters undressed without farther words. After they had gone to bed, and the light had been put out, the sound of Evelina's weeping came to Ann Eliza in the darkness, but she lay motionless on her own side of the bed, out of contact with her sister's shaken body. Never had she felt so coldly remote from Evelina.

The hours of the night moved slowly, ticked off with wearisome insistence by the clock which had played so prominent a part in their lives. Evelina's sobs still stirred the bed at gradually lengthening intervals, till at length Ann Eliza thought she slept. But with the dawn the eyes of the sisters met, and Ann Eliza's courage failed her as she looked in Evelina's face.

She sat up in bed and put out a pleading hand.

"Don't cry so, dearie. Don't."

"Oh, I can't bear it, I can't bear it," Evelina moaned.

Ann Eliza stroked her quivering shoulder. "Don't, don't," she repeated. "If you take the other hundred, won't that be enough? I always meant to give it to you. On'y I didn't want to tell you till your wedding day."

CHAPTER IX

Evelina's marriage took place on the appointed day. It was celebrated in the evening, in the chantry of the church which the sisters attended, and after it was over the few guests who had been present repaired to the Bunner Sisters' basement, where a wedding supper awaited them. Ann Eliza, aided by Miss Mellins and Mrs. Hawkins, and consciously supported by the sentimental interest of the whole street, had expended her utmost energy on the decoration of the shop and the back room. On the table a vase of white chrysanthemums stood between a dish of oranges and bananas and an iced wedding-cake wreathed with orange-blossoms of the bride's own making. Autumn leaves studded with paper roses festooned the what-not and the chromo of the Rock of Ages, and a wreath of yellow immortelles was twined about the clock which Evelina revered as the mysterious agent of her happiness.

At the table sat Miss Mellins, profusely spangled and bangled, her head sewing-girl, a pale young thing who had helped with Evelina's outfit, Mr. and Mrs. Hawkins, with Johnny, their eldest boy, and Mrs. Hochmuller and her daughter.

Mrs. Hochmuller's large blonde personality seemed to pervade the room to the effacement of the less amply-proportioned guests. It was rendered more impressive by a dress of crimson poplin that stood out from her in organ-like folds; and Linda, whom Ann Eliza had remembered as an uncouth child with a sly look about the eyes, surprised her by a sudden blossoming into feminine grace such as sometimes follows on a gawky girlhood. The Hochmullers, in fact, struck the dominant note in the entertainment. Beside them Evelina, unusually pale in her grey cashmere and white bonnet, looked like a faintly washed sketch beside a brilliant chromo; and Mr. Ramy, doomed to the traditional insignificance of the bridegroom's part, made no attempt to rise above his situation. Even Miss Mellins sparkled and jingled in vain in the shadow of Mrs. Hochmuller's crimson bulk; and Ann Eliza, with a sense of vague foreboding, saw that the wedding feast centred about the two guests she had most wished to exclude from it. What was said or done while they all sat about the table she never afterward recalled: the long hours remained in her memory as a whirl of high colours and loud voices, from which the pale presence of Evelina now and then emerged like a drowned face on a sunset-dabbled sea.

The next morning Mr. Ramy and his wife started for St. Louis, and Ann Eliza was left alone. Outwardly the first strain of parting was tempered by the arrival of Miss Mellins, Mrs. Hawkins and Johnny, who dropped in to help in the ungarlanding and tidying up of the back room. Ann Eliza was duly grateful for their kindness, but the "talking over" on which they had evidently counted was Dead Sea fruit on her lips; and just beyond the familiar warmth of their presences she saw the form of Solitude at her door.

Ann Eliza was but a small person to harbour so great a guest, and a trembling sense of insufficiency possessed her. She had no high musings to offer to the new companion of her hearth. Every one of her thoughts had hitherto turned to Evelina and shaped itself in homely easy words; of the mighty speech of silence she knew not the earliest syllable.

Everything in the back room and the shop, on the second day after Evelina's going, seemed to have grown coldly unfamiliar. The whole aspect of the place had changed with the changed conditions of Ann Eliza's life. The first customer who opened the shop-door startled her like a ghost; and all night she lay tossing on her side of the bed, sinking now and then into an uncertain doze from which she would suddenly wake to reach out her hand for Evelina. In the new silence surrounding her the walls and furniture found voice, frightening her at dusk and midnight with strange sighs and stealthy whispers. Ghostly hands shook the window shutters or rattled at the outer latch, and once she grew cold at the sound of a step like Evelina's stealing through the dark shop to die out on the threshold. In time, of course, she found an explanation for these noises, telling herself that the bedstead was warping, that Miss Mellins trod heavily overhead, or that the thunder of passing beer-waggons shook the door-latch; but the hours leading up to these conclusions were full of the floating terrors that harden into fixed foreboding. Worst of all were the solitary meals, when she absently continued to set aside the largest slice of pie for Evelina, and to let the tea grow cold while she waited for her sister to help herself to the first cup. Miss Mellins, coming in on one of these sad repasts, suggested the acquisition of a cat; but Ann Eliza shook her head. She had never been used to animals, and she felt the vague shrinking of the pious from creatures divided from her by the abyss of soullessness.

At length, after ten empty days, Evelina's first letter came.

"MY DEAR SISTER," she wrote, in her pinched Spencerian hand, "it seems strange to be in this great City so far from home alone with him I have chosen for life, but marriage has its solemn duties which those who are not can never hope to understand, and happier perhaps for this reason, life for them has only simple tasks and pleasures, but those who must take thought for others must be prepared to do their duty in whatever station it has pleased the Almighty to call them. Not that I have cause to complain, my dear Husband is all love and devotion, but being absent all day at his business how can I help but feel lonesome at times, as the poet says it is hard for they that love to live apart, and I often wonder, my dear Sister, how you are getting along alone in the store, may you never experience the feelings of solitude I have underwent since I came here. We are boarding now, but soon expect to find rooms and change our place of Residence, then I shall have all the care of a household to bear, but such is the fate of those who join their Lot with others, they cannot hope to escape from the burdens of Life, nor would I ask it, I would not live alway but while I live would always pray for strength to do my duty. This city is not near as large or handsome as New York, but had my lot been cast in a Wilderness I hope I should not repine, such never was my nature, and they who exchange their independence for the sweet name of Wife must be prepared to find all is not gold that glitters, nor I would not expect like you to drift down the stream of Life unfettered and serene as a Summer cloud, such is not my fate, but come what may will always find in me a resigned and prayerful Spirit, and hoping this finds you as well as it leaves me, I remain, my dear Sister,

"Yours truly,

"EVELINA B. RAMY."

Ann Eliza had always secretly admired the oratorical and impersonal tone of Evelina's letters; but the few she had previously read, having been addressed to school-mates or distant relatives, had appeared in the light of literary compositions rather than as records of personal experience. Now she could not but wish that Evelina had laid aside her swelling periods for a style more suited to the chronicling of homely incidents. She read the letter again and again, seeking for a clue to what her sister was really doing and thinking; but after each reading she emerged impressed but unenlightened from the labyrinth of Evelina's eloquence.

During the early winter she received two or three more letters of the same kind, each enclosing in its loose husk of rhetoric a smaller kernel of fact. By dint of patient interlinear study, Ann Eliza gathered from them that Evelina and her husband, after various costly experiments in boarding, had been reduced to a tenement-house flat; that living in St. Louis was more expensive than they had supposed, and that Mr. Ramy was kept out late at night (why, at a jeweller's, Ann Eliza wondered?) and found his position less satisfactory than he had been led to expect. Toward February the letters fell off; and finally they ceased to come.

At first Ann Eliza wrote, shyly but persistently, entreating for more frequent news; then, as one appeal after another was swallowed up in the mystery of Evelina's protracted silence, vague fears began to assail the elder sister. Perhaps Evelina was ill, and with no one to nurse her but a man who could not even make himself a cup of tea! Ann Eliza recalled the layer of dust in Mr. Ramy's shop, and pictures of domestic disorder mingled with the more poignant vision of her sister's illness. But surely if Evelina were ill Mr. Ramy would have written. He wrote a small neat hand, and epistolary communication was not an insuperable embarrassment to him. The too probable alternative was that both the unhappy pair had been prostrated by some disease which left them powerless to summon her—for summon her they surely would, Ann Eliza with unconscious cynicism reflected, if she or her small economies could be of use to them! The more she strained her eyes into the mystery, the darker it grew; and her lack of initiative, her inability to imagine what steps might be taken to trace the lost in distant places, left her benumbed and helpless.

At last there floated up from some depth of troubled memory the name of the firm of St. Louis jewellers by whom Mr. Ramy was employed. After much hesitation, and considerable effort, she addressed to them a timid request for news of her brother-in-law; and sooner than she could have hoped the answer reached her.

"DEAR MADAM,

"In reply to yours of the 29th ult. we beg to state the party you refer to was discharged from our employ a month ago. We are sorry we are unable to furnish you wish his address.

"Yours Respectfully,

"LUDWIG AND HAMMERBUSCH."

Ann Eliza read and re-read the curt statement in a stupor of distress. She had lost her last trace of Evelina. All that night she lay awake, revolving the stupendous project of going to St. Louis in search of her sister; but though she pieced together her few financial possibilities with the ingenuity of a brain used to fitting odd scraps into patch-work quilts, she woke to the cold daylight fact that she could not raise the money for her fare. Her wedding gift to Evelina had left her without any resources beyond her daily earnings, and these had steadily dwindled as the winter passed. She had long since renounced her weekly visit to the butcher, and had reduced her other expenses to the narrowest measure; but the most systematic frugality had not enabled her to put by any money. In spite of her dogged efforts to maintain the prosperity of the little shop, her sister's absence had already told on its business. Now that Ann Eliza had to carry the bundles to the dyer's herself, the customers who called in her absence, finding the shop locked, too often went elsewhere. Moreover, after several stern but unavailing efforts, she had had to give up the trimming of bonnets, which in Evelina's hands had been the most lucrative as well as the most interesting part of the business. This change, to the passing female eye, robbed the shop window of its chief attraction; and when painful experience had convinced the regular customers of the Bunner Sisters of Ann Eliza's lack of millinery skill they began to lose faith in her ability to curl a feather or even "freshen up" a bunch of flowers. The time came when Ann Eliza had almost made up her mind to speak to the lady with puffed sleeves, who had always looked at her so kindly, and had once ordered a hat of Evelina. Perhaps the lady with puffed sleeves would be able to get her a little plain sewing to do; or she might recommend the shop to friends. Ann Eliza, with this possibility in view, rummaged out of a drawer the fly-blown remainder of the business cards which the sisters had ordered in the first flush of their commercial adventure; but when the lady with puffed sleeves finally appeared she was in deep mourning, and wore so sad a look that Ann Eliza dared not speak. She came in to buy some spools of black thread and silk, and in the doorway she turned back to say: "I am going away to-morrow for a long time. I hope you will have a pleasant winter." And the door shut on her.

One day not long after this it occurred to Ann Eliza to go to Hoboken in quest of Mrs. Hochmuller. Much as she shrank from pouring her distress into that particular ear, her anxiety had carried her beyond such reluctance; but when she began to think the matter over she was faced by a new difficulty. On the occasion of her only visit to Mrs. Hochmuller, she and Evelina had suffered themselves to be led there by Mr. Ramy; and Ann Eliza now perceived that she did not even know the name of the laundress's suburb, much less that of the street in which she lived. But she must have news of Evelina, and no obstacle was great enough to thwart her.

Though she longed to turn to some one for advice she disliked to expose her situation to Miss Mellins's searching eye, and at first she could think of no other confidant. Then she remembered Mrs. Hawkins, or rather her husband, who, though Ann Eliza had always thought him a dull uneducated man, was probably gifted with the mysterious masculine faculty of finding out people's addresses. It went hard with Ann Eliza to trust her secret even to the mild ear of Mrs. Hawkins, but at least she was spared the cross-examination to which the dress-maker would have subjected her. The accumulating pressure of domestic cares had so crushed in Mrs. Hawkins any curiosity concerning the affairs of others that she received her visitor's confidence with an almost masculine indifference, while she rocked her teething baby on one arm and with the other tried to check the acrobatic impulses of the next in age.

"My, my," she simply said as Ann Eliza ended. "Keep still now, Arthur: Miss Bunner don't want you to jump up and down on her foot to-day. And what are you gaping at, Johnny? Run right off and play," she added, turning sternly to her eldest, who, because he was the least naughty, usually bore the brunt of her wrath against the others.

"Well, perhaps Mr. Hawkins can help you," Mrs. Hawkins continued meditatively, while the children, after scattering at her bidding, returned to their previous pursuits like flies settling down on the spot from which an exasperated hand has swept them. "I'll send him right round the minute he comes in, and you can tell him the whole story. I wouldn't wonder but what he can find that Mrs. Hochmuller's address in the d'rectory. I know they've got one where he works."

"I'd be real thankful if he could," Ann Eliza murmured, rising from her seat with the factitious sense of lightness that comes from imparting a long-hidden dread.

CHAPTER X

Mr. Hawkins proved himself worthy of his wife's faith in his capacity. He learned from Ann Eliza as much as she could tell him about Mrs. Hochmuller and returned the next evening with a scrap of paper bearing her address, beneath which Johnny (the family scribe) had written in a large round hand the names of the streets that led there from the ferry.

Ann Eliza lay awake all that night, repeating over and over again the directions Mr. Hawkins had given her. He was a kind man, and she knew he would willingly have gone with her to Hoboken; indeed she read in his timid eye the half-formed intention of offering to accompany her—but on such an errand she preferred to go alone.

The next Sunday, accordingly, she set out early, and without much trouble found her way to the ferry. Nearly a year had passed since her previous visit to Mrs. Hochmuller, and a chilly April breeze smote her face as she stepped on the boat. Most of the passengers were huddled together in the cabin, and Ann Eliza shrank into its obscurest corner, shivering under the thin black mantle which had seemed so hot in July. She began to feel a little bewildered as she stepped ashore, but a paternal policeman put her into the right car, and as in a dream she found herself retracing the way to Mrs. Hochmuller's door. She had told the conductor the name of the street at which she wished to get out, and presently she stood in the biting wind at the corner near the beer-saloon, where the sun had once beat down on her so fiercely. At length an empty car appeared, its yellow flank emblazoned with the name of Mrs. Hochmuller's suburb, and Ann Eliza was presently jolting past the narrow brick houses islanded between vacant lots like giant piles in a desolate lagoon. When the car reached the end of its journey she got out and stood for some time trying to remember which turn Mr. Ramy had taken. She had just made up her mind to ask the car-driver when he shook the reins on the backs of his lean horses, and the car, still empty, jogged away toward Hoboken.

Ann Eliza, left alone by the roadside, began to move cautiously forward, looking about for a small red house with a gable overhung by an elm-tree; but everything about her seemed unfamiliar and forbidding. One or two surly looking men slouched past with inquisitive glances, and she could not make up her mind to stop and speak to them.

At length a tow-headed boy came out of a swinging door suggestive of illicit conviviality, and to him Ann Eliza ventured to confide her difficulty. The offer of five cents fired him with an instant willingness to lead her to Mrs. Hochmuller, and he was soon trotting past the stone-cutter's yard with Ann Eliza in his wake.

Another turn in the road brought them to the little red house, and having rewarded her guide Ann Eliza unlatched the gate and walked up to the door. Her heart was beating violently, and she had to lean against the door-post to compose her twitching lips: she had not known till that moment how much it was going to hurt her to speak of Evelina to Mrs. Hochmuller. As her agitation subsided she began to notice how much the appearance of the house had changed. It was not only that winter had stripped the elm, and blackened the flower-borders: the house itself had a debased and deserted air. The window-panes were cracked and dirty, and one or two shutters swung dismally on loosened hinges.

She rang several times before the door was opened. At length an Irish woman with a shawl over her head and a baby in her arms appeared on the threshold, and glancing past her into the narrow passage Ann Eliza saw that Mrs. Hochmuller's neat abode had deteriorated as much within as without.

At the mention of the name the woman stared. "Mrs. who, did ye say?"

"Mrs. Hochmuller. This is surely her house?"

"No, it ain't neither," said the woman turning away.

"Oh, but wait, please," Ann Eliza entreated. "I can't be mistaken. I mean the Mrs. Hochmuller who takes in washing. I came out to see her last June."

"Oh, the Dutch washerwoman is it—her that used to live here? She's been gone two months and more. It's Mike McNulty lives here now. Whisht!" to the baby, who had squared his mouth for a howl.

Ann Eliza's knees grew weak. "Mrs. Hochmuller gone? But where has she gone? She must be somewhere round here. Can't you tell me?"

"Sure an' I can't," said the woman. "She wint away before iver we come."

"Dalia Geoghegan, will ye bring the choild in out av the cowld?" cried an irate voice from within.

"Please wait—oh, please wait," Ann Eliza insisted. "You see I must find Mrs. Hochmuller."

"Why don't ye go and look for her thin?" the woman returned, slamming the door in her face.

She stood motionless on the door-step, dazed by the immensity of her disappointment, till a burst of loud voices inside the house drove her down the path and out of the gate.

Even then she could not grasp what had happened, and pausing in the road she looked back at the house, half hoping that Mrs. Hochmuller's once detested face might appear at one of the grimy windows.

She was roused by an icy wind that seemed to spring up suddenly from the desolate scene, piercing her thin dress like gauze; and turning away she began to retrace her steps. She thought of enquiring for Mrs. Hochmuller at some of the neighbouring houses, but their look was so unfriendly that she walked on without making up her mind at which door to ring.

When she reached the horse-car terminus a car was just moving off toward Hoboken, and for nearly an hour she had to wait on the corner in the bitter wind. Her hands and feet were stiff with cold when the car at length loomed into sight again, and she thought of stopping somewhere on the way to the ferry for a cup of tea; but before the region of lunch-rooms was reached she had grown so sick and dizzy that the thought of food was repulsive. At length she found herself on the ferry-boat, in the soothing stuffiness of the crowded cabin; then came another interval of shivering on a street-corner, another long jolting journey in a "cross-town" car that smelt of damp straw and tobacco; and lastly, in the cold spring dusk, she unlocked her door and groped her way through the shop to her fireless bedroom.

The next morning Mrs. Hawkins, dropping in to hear the result of the trip, found Ann Eliza sitting behind the counter wrapped in an old shawl.

"Why, Miss Bunner, you're sick! You must have fever—your face is just as red!"

"It's nothing. I guess I caught cold yesterday on the ferry-boat," Ann Eliza acknowledged.

"And it's jest like a vault in here!" Mrs. Hawkins rebuked her. "Let me feel your hand—it's burning. Now, Miss Bunner, you've got to go right to bed this very minute."

"Oh, but I can't, Mrs. Hawkins." Ann Eliza attempted a wan smile. "You forget there ain't nobody but me to tend the store."

"I guess you won't tend it long neither, if you ain't careful," Mrs. Hawkins grimly rejoined. Beneath her placid exterior she cherished a morbid passion for disease and death, and the sight of Ann Eliza's suffering had roused her from her habitual indifference. "There ain't so many folks comes to the store anyhow," she went on with unconscious cruelty, "and I'll go right up and see if Miss Mellins can't spare one of her girls."

Ann Eliza, too weary to resist, allowed Mrs. Hawkins to put her to bed and make a cup of tea over the stove, while Miss Mellins, always good-naturedly responsive to any appeal for help, sent down the weak-eyed little girl to deal with hypothetical customers.

Ann Eliza, having so far abdicated her independence, sank into sudden apathy. As far as she could remember, it was the first time in her life that she had been taken care of instead of taking care, and there was a momentary relief in the surrender. She swallowed the tea like an obedient child, allowed a poultice to be applied to her aching chest and uttered no protest when a fire was kindled in the rarely used grate; but as Mrs. Hawkins bent over to "settle" her pillows she raised herself on her elbow to whisper: "Oh, Mrs. Hawkins, Mrs. Hochmuller warn't there." The tears rolled down her cheeks.

"She warn't there? Has she moved?"

"Over two months ago—and they don't know where she's gone. Oh what'll I do, Mrs. Hawkins?"

"There, there, Miss Bunner. You lay still and don't fret. I'll ask Mr. Hawkins soon as ever he comes home."

Ann Eliza murmured her gratitude, and Mrs. Hawkins, bending down, kissed her on the forehead. "Don't you fret," she repeated, in the voice with which she soothed her children.

For over a week Ann Eliza lay in bed, faithfully nursed by her two neighbours, while the weak-eyed child, and the pale sewing girl who had helped to finish Evelina's wedding dress, took turns in minding the shop. Every morning, when her friends appeared, Ann Eliza lifted her head to ask: "Is there a letter?" and at their gentle negative sank back in silence. Mrs. Hawkins, for several days, spoke no more of her promise to consult her husband as to the best way of tracing Mrs. Hochmuller; and dread of fresh disappointment kept Ann Eliza from bringing up the subject.

But the following Sunday evening, as she sat for the first time bolstered up in her rocking-chair near the stove, while Miss Mellins studied the Police Gazette beneath the lamp, there came a knock on the shop-door and Mr. Hawkins entered.

Ann Eliza's first glance at his plain friendly face showed her he had news to give, but though she no longer attempted to hide her anxiety from Miss Mellins, her lips trembled too much to let her speak.

"Good evening, Miss Bunner," said Mr. Hawkins in his dragging voice. "I've been over to Hoboken all day looking round for Mrs. Hochmuller."

"Oh, Mr. Hawkins—you *have*?"

"I made a thorough search, but I'm sorry to say it was no use. She's left Hoboken—moved clear away, and nobody seems to know where."

"It was real good of you, Mr. Hawkins." Ann Eliza's voice struggled up in a faint whisper through the submerging tide of her disappointment.

Mr. Hawkins, in his embarrassed sense of being the bringer of bad news, stood before her uncertainly; then he turned to go. "No trouble at all," he paused to assure her from the doorway.

She wanted to speak again, to detain him, to ask him to advise her; but the words caught in her throat and she lay back silent.

The next day she got up early, and dressed and bonneted herself with twitching fingers. She waited till the weak-eyed child appeared, and having laid on her minute instructions as to the care of the shop, she slipped out into the street. It had occurred to her in one of the weary watches of the previous night that she might go to Tiffany's and make enquiries about Ramy's past. Possibly in that way she might obtain some information that would suggest a new way of reaching Evelina. She was guiltily aware that Mrs. Hawkins and Miss Mellins would be angry with her for venturing out of doors, but she knew she should never feel any better till she had news of Evelina.

The morning air was sharp, and as she turned to face the wind she felt so weak and unsteady that she wondered if she should ever get as far as Union Square; but by walking very slowly, and standing still now and then when she could do so without being noticed, she found herself at last before the jeweller's great glass doors.

It was still so early that there were no purchasers in the shop, and she felt herself the centre of innumerable unemployed eyes as she moved forward between long lines of show-cases glittering with diamonds and silver.

She was glancing about in the hope of finding the clock-department without having to approach one of the impressive gentlemen who paced the empty aisles, when she attracted the attention of one of the most impressive of the number.

The formidable benevolence with which he enquired what he could do for her made her almost despair of explaining herself; but she finally disentangled from a flurry of wrong beginnings the request to be shown to the clock-department.

The gentleman considered her thoughtfully. "May I ask what style of clock you are looking for? Would it be for a wedding-present, or—?"

The irony of the allusion filled Ann Eliza's veins with sudden strength. "I don't want to buy a clock at all. I want to see the head of the department."

"Mr. Loomis?" His stare still weighed her—then he seemed to brush aside the problem she presented as beneath his notice. "Oh, certainly. Take the elevator to the second floor. Next aisle to the left." He waved her down the endless perspective of show-cases.

Ann Eliza followed the line of his lordly gesture, and a swift ascent brought her to a great hall full of the buzzing and booming of thousands of clocks. Whichever way she looked, clocks stretched away from her in glittering interminable vistas: clocks of all sizes and voices, from the bell-throated giant of the hallway to the chirping dressing-table toy; tall clocks of mahogany and brass with cathedral chimes; clocks of bronze, glass, porcelain, of every possible size, voice and configuration; and between their serried ranks, along the polished floor of the aisles, moved the languid forms of other gentlemanly floor-walkers, waiting for their duties to begin.

One of them soon approached, and Ann Eliza repeated her request. He received it affably.

"Mr. Loomis? Go right down to the office at the other end." He pointed to a kind of box of ground glass and highly polished panelling.

As she thanked him he turned to one of his companions and said something in which she caught the name of Mr. Loomis, and which was received with an appreciative chuckle. She suspected herself of being the object of the pleasantry, and straightened her thin shoulders under her mantle.

The door of the office stood open, and within sat a gray-bearded man at a desk. He looked up kindly, and again she asked for Mr. Loomis.

"I'm Mr. Loomis. What can I do for you?"

He was much less portentous than the others, though she guessed him to be above them in authority; and encouraged by his tone she seated herself on the edge of the chair he waved her to.

"I hope you'll excuse my troubling you, sir. I came to ask if you could tell me anything about Mr. Herman Ramy. He was employed here in the clock-department two or three years ago."

Mr. Loomis showed no recognition of the name.

"Ramy? When was he discharged?"

"I don't har'ly know. He was very sick, and when he got well his place had been filled. He married my sister last October and they went to St. Louis, I ain't had any news of them for over two months, and she's my only sister, and I'm most crazy worrying about her."

"I see." Mr. Loomis reflected. "In what capacity was Ramy employed here?" he asked after a moment.

"He—he told us that he was one of the heads of the clock-department," Ann Eliza stammered, overswept by a sudden doubt.

"That was probably a slight exaggeration. But I can tell you about him by referring to our books. The name again?"

"Ramy—Herman Ramy."

There ensued a long silence, broken only by the flutter of leaves as Mr. Loomis turned over his ledgers. Presently he looked up, keeping his finger between the pages.

"Here it is—Herman Ramy. He was one of our ordinary workmen, and left us three years and a half ago last June."

"On account of sickness?" Ann Eliza faltered.

Mr. Loomis appeared to hesitate; then he said: "I see no mention of sickness." Ann Eliza felt his compassionate eyes on her again. "Perhaps I'd better tell you the truth. He was discharged for drug-taking. A capable workman, but we couldn't keep him straight. I'm sorry to have to tell you this, but it seems fairer, since you say you're anxious about your sister."

The polished sides of the office vanished from Ann Eliza's sight, and the cackle of the innumerable clocks came to her like the yell of waves in a storm. She tried to speak but could not; tried to get to her feet, but the floor was gone.

"I'm very sorry," Mr. Loomis repeated, closing the ledger. "I remember the man perfectly now. He used to disappear every now and then, and turn up again in a state that made him useless for days."

As she listened, Ann Eliza recalled the day when she had come on Mr. Ramy sitting in abject dejection behind his counter. She saw again the blurred unrecognizing eyes he had raised to her, the layer of dust over everything in the shop, and the green bronze clock in the window representing a Newfoundland dog with his paw on a book. She stood up slowly.

"Thank you. I'm sorry to have troubled you."

"It was no trouble. You say Ramy married your sister last October?"

"Yes, sir; and they went to St. Louis right afterward. I don't know how to find her. I thought maybe somebody here might know about him."

"Well, possibly some of the workmen might. Leave me your name and I'll send you word if I get on his track."

He handed her a pencil, and she wrote down her address; then she walked away blindly between the clocks.

CHAPTER XI

Mr. Loomis, true to his word, wrote a few days later that he had enquired in vain in the work-shop for any news of Ramy; and as she folded this letter and laid it between the leaves of her Bible, Ann Eliza felt that her last hope was gone. Miss Mellins, of course, had long since suggested the mediation of the police, and cited from her favourite literature convincing instances of the supernatural ability of the Pinkerton detective; but Mr. Hawkins, when called in council, dashed this project by remarking that detectives cost something like twenty dollars a day; and a vague fear of the law, some half-formed vision of Evelina in the clutch of a blue-coated "officer," kept Ann Eliza from invoking the aid of the police.

After the arrival of Mr. Loomis's note the weeks followed each other uneventfully. Ann Eliza's cough clung to her till late in the spring, the reflection in her looking-glass grew more bent and meagre, and her forehead sloped back farther toward the twist of hair that was fastened above her parting by a comb of black India-rubber.

Toward spring a lady who was expecting a baby took up her abode at the Mendoza Family Hotel, and through the friendly intervention of Miss Mellins the making of some of the baby-clothes was entrusted to Ann Eliza. This eased her of anxiety for the immediate future; but she had to rouse herself to feel any sense of relief. Her personal welfare was what least concerned her. Sometimes she thought of giving up the shop altogether; and only the fear that, if she changed her address, Evelina might not be able to find her, kept her from carrying out this plan.

Since she had lost her last hope of tracing her sister, all the activities of her lonely imagination had been concentrated on the possibility of Evelina's coming back to her. The discovery of Ramy's secret filled her with dreadful fears. In the solitude of the shop and the back room she was tortured by vague pictures of Evelina's sufferings. What horrors might not be hidden beneath her silence? Ann Eliza's great dread was that Miss Mellins should worm out of her what she had learned from Mr. Loomis. She was sure Miss Mellins must have abominable things to tell about drug-fiends—things she did not have the strength to hear. "Drug-fiend"—the very word was Satanic; she could hear Miss Mellins roll it on her tongue. But Ann Eliza's own imagination, left to itself, had begun to people the long hours with evil visions. Sometimes, in the night, she thought she heard herself called: the voice was her sister's, but faint with a nameless terror. Her most peaceful moments were those in which she managed to convince herself that Evelina was dead. She thought of her then, mournfully but more calmly, as thrust away under the neglected mound of some unknown cemetery, where no headstone marked her name, no mourner with flowers for another grave paused in pity to lay a blossom on hers. But this vision did not often give Ann Eliza its negative relief; and always, beneath its hazy lines, lurked the dark conviction that Evelina was alive, in misery and longing for her.

So the summer wore on. Ann Eliza was conscious that Mrs. Hawkins and Miss Mellins were watching her with affectionate anxiety, but the knowledge brought no comfort. She no longer cared what they felt or thought about her. Her grief lay far beyond touch of human healing, and after a while she became aware that they knew they could not help her. They still came in as often as their busy lives permitted, but their visits grew shorter, and Mrs. Hawkins always brought Arthur or the baby, so that there should be something to talk about, and some one whom she could scold.

The autumn came, and the winter. Business had fallen off again, and but few purchasers came to the little shop in the basement. In January Ann Eliza pawned her mother's cashmere scarf, her mosaic brooch, and the rosewood what-not on which the clock had always stood; she would have sold the bedstead too, but for the persistent vision of Evelina returning weak and weary, and not knowing where to lay her head.

The winter passed in its turn, and March reappeared with its galaxies of yellow jonquils at the windy street corners, reminding Ann Eliza of the spring day when Evelina had come home with a bunch of jonquils in her hand. In spite of the flowers which lent such a premature brightness to the streets the month was fierce and stormy, and Ann Eliza could get no warmth into her bones. Nevertheless, she was insensibly beginning to take up the healing routine of life. Little by little she had grown used to being alone, she had begun to take a languid interest in the one or two new purchasers the season had brought, and though the thought of Evelina was as poignant as ever, it was less persistently in the foreground of her mind.

Late one afternoon she was sitting behind the counter, wrapped in her shawl, and wondering how soon she might draw down the blinds and retreat into the comparative cosiness of the back room. She was not thinking of anything in particular, except perhaps in a hazy way of the lady with the puffed sleeves, who after her long eclipse had reappeared the day before in sleeves of a new cut, and bought some tape and needles. The lady still wore mourning, but she was evidently lightening it, and Ann Eliza saw in this the hope of future orders. The lady had left the shop about an hour before, walking away with her graceful step toward Fifth Avenue. She had wished Ann Eliza good day in her usual affable way, and Ann Eliza thought how odd it was that they should have been acquainted so long, and yet that she should not know the lady's name. From this consideration her mind wandered to the cut of the lady's new sleeves, and she was vexed with herself for not having noted it more carefully. She felt Miss Mellins might have liked to know about it. Ann Eliza's powers of observation had never been as keen as Evelina's, when the latter was not too self-absorbed to exert them. As Miss Mellins always said, Evelina could "take patterns with her eyes": she could have cut that new sleeve out of a folded newspaper in a trice! Musing on these things, Ann Eliza wished the lady would come back and give her another look at the sleeve. It was not unlikely that she might pass that way, for she certainly lived in or about the Square. Suddenly Ann Eliza remarked a small neat handkerchief on the counter: it must have dropped from the lady's purse, and she would probably come back to get it. Ann Eliza, pleased at the idea, sat on behind the counter and watched the darkening street. She always lit the gas as late as possible, keeping the box of matches at her elbow, so that if any one came she could apply a quick flame to the gas-jet. At length through the deepening dusk she distinguished a slim dark figure coming down the steps to the shop. With a little warmth of pleasure about her heart she reached up to light the gas. "I do believe I'll ask her name this time," she thought. She raised the flame to its full height, and saw her sister standing in the door.

There she was at last, the poor pale shade of Evelina, her thin face blanched of its faint pink, the stiff ripples gone from her hair, and a mantle shabbier than Ann Eliza's drawn about her narrow shoulders. The glare of the gas beat full on her as she stood and looked at Ann Eliza.

"Sister—oh, Evelina! I knowed you'd come!"

Ann Eliza had caught her close with a long moan of triumph. Vague words poured from her as she laid her cheek against Evelina's—trivial inarticulate endearments caught from Mrs. Hawkins's long discourses to her baby.

For a while Evelina let herself be passively held; then she drew back from her sister's clasp and looked about the shop. "I'm dead tired. Ain't there any fire?" she asked.

"Of course there is!" Ann Eliza, holding her hand fast, drew her into the back room. She did not want to ask any questions yet: she simply wanted to feel the emptiness of the room brimmed full again by the one presence that was warmth and light to her.

She knelt down before the grate, scraped some bits of coal and kindling from the bottom of the coal-scuttle, and drew one of the rocking-chairs up to the weak flame. "There—that'll blaze up in a minute," she said. She pressed Evelina down on the faded cushions of the rocking-chair, and, kneeling beside her, began to rub her hands.

"You're stone-cold, ain't you? Just sit still and warm yourself while I run and get the kettle. I've got something you always used to fancy for supper." She laid her hand on Evelina's shoulder. "Don't talk—oh, don't talk yet!" she implored. She wanted to keep that one frail second of happiness between herself and what she knew must come.

Evelina, without a word, bent over the fire, stretching her thin hands to the blaze and watching Ann Eliza fill the kettle and set the supper table. Her gaze had the dreamy fixity of a half-awakened child's.

Ann Eliza, with a smile of triumph, brought a slice of custard pie from the cupboard and put it by her sister's plate.

"You do like that, don't you? Miss Mellins sent it down to me this morning. She had her aunt from Brooklyn to dinner. Ain't it funny it just so happened?"

"I ain't hungry," said Evelina, rising to approach the table.

She sat down in her usual place, looked about her with the same wondering stare, and then, as of old, poured herself out the first cup of tea.

"Where's the what-not gone to?" she suddenly asked.

Ann Eliza set down the teapot and rose to get a spoon from the cupboard. With her back to the room she said: "The what-not? Why, you see, dearie, living here all alone by myself it only made one more thing to dust; so I sold it."

Evelina's eyes were still travelling about the familiar room. Though it was against all the traditions of the Bunner family to sell any household possession, she showed no surprise at her sister's answer.

"And the clock? The clock's gone too."

"Oh, I gave that away—I gave it to Mrs. Hawkins. She's kep' awake so nights with that last baby."

"I wish you'd never bought it," said Evelina harshly.

Ann Eliza's heart grew faint with fear. Without answering, she crossed over to her sister's seat and poured her out a second cup of tea. Then another thought struck her, and she went back to the cupboard and took out the cordial. In Evelina's absence considerable draughts had been drawn from it by invalid neighbours; but a glassful of the precious liquid still remained.

"Here, drink this right off—it'll warm you up quicker than anything," Ann Eliza said.

Evelina obeyed, and a slight spark of colour came into her cheeks. She turned to the custard pie and began to eat with a silent voracity distressing to watch. She did not even look to see what was left for Ann Eliza.

"I ain't hungry," she said at last as she laid down her fork. "I'm only so dead tired—that's the trouble."

"Then you'd better get right into bed. Here's my old plaid dressing-gown—you remember it, don't you?" Ann Eliza laughed, recalling Evelina's ironies on the subject of the antiquated garment. With trembling fingers she began to undo her sister's cloak. The dress beneath it told a tale of poverty that Ann Eliza dared not pause to note. She drew it gently off, and as it slipped from Evelina's shoulders it revealed a tiny black bag hanging on a ribbon about her neck. Evelina lifted her hand as though to screen the bag from Ann Eliza; and the elder sister, seeing the gesture, continued her task with lowered eyes. She undressed Evelina as quickly as she could, and wrapping her in the plaid dressing-gown put her to bed, and spread her own shawl and her sister's cloak above the blanket.

"Where's the old red comfortable?" Evelina asked, as she sank down on the pillow.

"The comfortable? Oh, it was so hot and heavy I never used it after you went—so I sold that too. I never could sleep under much clothes."

She became aware that her sister was looking at her more attentively.

"I guess you've been in trouble too," Evelina said.

"Me? In trouble? What do you mean, Evelina?"

"You've had to pawn the things, I suppose," Evelina continued in a weary unmoved tone. "Well, I've been through worse than that. I've been to hell and back."

"Oh, Evelina—don't say it, sister!" Ann Eliza implored, shrinking from the unholy word. She knelt down and began to rub her sister's feet beneath the bedclothes.

"I've been to hell and back—if I *am* back," Evelina repeated. She lifted her head from the pillow and began to talk with a sudden feverish volubility. "It began right away, less than a month after we were married. I've been in hell all that time, Ann Eliza." She fixed her eyes with passionate intentness on Ann Eliza's face. "He took opium. I didn't find it out till long afterward—at first, when he acted so strange, I thought he drank. But it was worse, much worse than drinking."

"Oh, sister, don't say it—don't say it yet! It's so sweet just to have you here with me again."

"I must say it," Evelina insisted, her flushed face burning with a kind of bitter cruelty. "You don't know what life's like—you don't know anything about it—setting here safe all the while in this peaceful place."

"Oh, Evelina—why didn't you write and send for me if it was like that?"

"That's why I couldn't write. Didn't you guess I was ashamed?"

"How could you be? Ashamed to write to Ann Eliza?"

Evelina raised herself on her thin elbow, while Ann Eliza, bending over, drew a corner of the shawl about her shoulder.

"Do lay down again. You'll catch your death."

"My death? That don't frighten me! You don't know what I've been through." And sitting upright in the old mahogany bed, with flushed cheeks and chattering teeth, and Ann Eliza's trembling arm clasping the shawl about her neck, Evelina poured out her story. It was a tale of misery and humiliation so remote from the elder sister's innocent experiences that much of it was hardly intelligible to her. Evelina's dreadful familiarity with it all, her fluency about things which Ann Eliza half-guessed and quickly shuddered back from, seemed even more alien and terrible than the actual tale she told. It was one thing—and heaven knew it was bad enough!—to learn that one's sister's husband was a drug-fiend; it was another, and much worse thing, to learn from that sister's pallid lips what vileness lay behind the word.

Evelina, unconscious of any distress but her own, sat upright, shivering in Ann Eliza's hold, while she piled up, detail by detail, her dreary narrative.

"The minute we got out there, and he found the job wasn't as good as he expected, he changed. At first I thought he was sick—I used to try to keep him home and nurse him. Then I saw it was something different. He used to go off for hours at a time, and when he came back his eyes kinder had a fog over them. Sometimes he didn't har'ly know me, and when he did he seemed to hate me. Once he hit me here." She touched her breast. "Do you remember, Ann Eliza, that time he didn't come to see us for a week—the time after we all went to Central Park together—and you and I thought he must be sick?"

Ann Eliza nodded.

"Well, that was the trouble—he'd been at it then. But nothing like as bad. After we'd been out there about a month he disappeared for a whole week. They took him back at the store, and gave him another chance; but the second time they discharged him, and he drifted round for ever so long before he could get another job. We spent all our money and had to move to a cheaper place. Then he got something to do, but they hardly paid him anything, and he didn't stay there long. When he found out about the baby—"

"The baby?" Ann Eliza faltered.

"It's dead—it only lived a day. When he found out about it, he got mad, and said he hadn't any money to pay doctors' bills, and I'd better write to you to help us. He had an idea you had money hidden away that I didn't know about." She turned to her sister with remorseful eyes. "It was him that made me get that hundred dollars out of you."

"Hush, hush. I always meant it for you anyhow."

"Yes, but I wouldn't have taken it if he hadn't been at me the whole time. He used to make me do just what he wanted. Well, when I said I wouldn't write to you for more money he said I'd better try and earn some myself. That was when he struck me.... Oh, you don't know what I'm talking about yet!... I tried to get work at a milliner's, but I was so sick I couldn't stay. I was sick all the time. I wisht I'd ha' died, Ann Eliza."

"No, no, Evelina."

"Yes, I do. It kept getting worse and worse. We pawned the furniture, and they turned us out because we couldn't pay the rent; and so then we went to board with Mrs. Hochmuller."

Ann Eliza pressed her closer to dissemble her own tremor. "Mrs. Hochmuller?"

"Didn't you know she was out there? She moved out a month after we did. She wasn't bad to me, and I think she tried to keep him straight—but Linda—"

"Linda—?"

"Well, when I kep' getting worse, and he was always off, for days at a time, the doctor had me sent to a hospital."

"A hospital? Sister—sister!"

"It was better than being with him; and the doctors were real kind to me. After the baby was born I was very sick and had to stay there a good while. And one day when I was laying there Mrs. Hochmuller came in as white as a sheet, and told me him and Linda had gone off together and taken all her money. That's the last I ever saw of him." She broke off with a laugh and began to cough again.

Ann Eliza tried to persuade her to lie down and sleep, but the rest of her story had to be told before she could be soothed into consent. After the news of Ramy's flight she had had brain fever, and had been sent to another hospital where she stayed a long time—how long she couldn't remember. Dates and days meant nothing to her in the shapeless ruin of her life. When she left the hospital she found that Mrs. Hochmuller had gone too. She was penniless, and had no one to turn to. A lady visitor at the hospital was kind, and found her a place where she did housework; but she was so weak they couldn't keep her. Then she got a job as waitress in a down-town lunch-room, but one day she fainted while she was handing a dish, and that evening when they paid her they told her she needn't come again.

"After that I begged in the streets"—(Ann Eliza's grasp again grew tight)—"and one afternoon last week, when the matinees was coming out, I met a man with a pleasant face, something like Mr. Hawkins, and he stopped and asked me what the trouble was. I told him if he'd give me five dollars I'd have money enough to buy a ticket back to New York, and he took a good look at me and said, well, if that was what I wanted he'd go straight to the station with me and give me the five dollars there. So he did—and he bought the ticket, and put me in the cars."

Evelina sank back, her face a sallow wedge in the white cleft of the pillow. Ann Eliza leaned over her, and for a long time they held each other without speaking.

They were still clasped in this dumb embrace when there was a step in the shop and Ann Eliza, starting up, saw Miss Mellins in the doorway.

"My sakes, Miss Bunner! What in the land are you doing? Miss Evelina—Mrs. Ramy—it ain't you?"

Miss Mellins's eyes, bursting from their sockets, sprang from Evelina's pallid face to the disordered supper table and the heap of worn clothes on the floor; then they turned back to Ann Eliza, who had placed herself on the defensive between her sister and the dress-maker.

"My sister Evelina has come back—come back on a visit. She was taken sick in the cars on the way home—I guess she caught cold—so I made her go right to bed as soon as ever she got here."

Ann Eliza was surprised at the strength and steadiness of her voice. Fortified by its sound she went on, her eyes on Miss Mellins's baffled countenance: "Mr. Ramy has gone west on a trip—a trip connected with his business; and Evelina is going to stay with me till he comes back."

CHAPTER XII

What measure of belief her explanation of Evelina's return obtained in the small circle of her friends Ann Eliza did not pause to enquire. Though she could not remember ever having told a lie before, she adhered with rigid tenacity to the consequences of her first lapse from truth, and fortified her original statement with additional details whenever a questioner sought to take her unawares.

But other and more serious burdens lay on her startled conscience. For the first time in her life she dimly faced the awful problem of the inutility of self-sacrifice. Hitherto she had never thought of questioning the inherited principles which had guided her life. Self-effacement for the good of others had always seemed to her both natural and necessary; but then she had taken it for granted that it implied the securing of that good. Now she perceived that to refuse the gifts of life does not ensure their transmission to those for whom they have been surrendered; and her familiar heaven was unpeopled. She felt she could no longer trust in the goodness of God, and there was only a black abyss above the roof of Bunner Sisters.

But there was little time to brood upon such problems. The care of Evelina filled Ann Eliza's days and nights. The hastily summoned doctor had pronounced her to be suffering from pneumonia, and under his care the first stress of the disease was relieved. But her recovery was only partial, and long after the doctor's visits had ceased she continued to lie in bed, too weak to move, and seemingly indifferent to everything about her.

At length one evening, about six weeks after her return, she said to her sister: "I don't feel's if I'd ever get up again."

Ann Eliza turned from the kettle she was placing on the stove. She was startled by the echo the words woke in her own breast.

"Don't you talk like that, Evelina! I guess you're on'y tired out—and disheartened."

"Yes, I'm disheartened," Evelina murmured.

A few months earlier Ann Eliza would have met the confession with a word of pious admonition; now she accepted it in silence.

"Maybe you'll brighten up when your cough gets better," she suggested.

"Yes—or my cough'll get better when I brighten up," Evelina retorted with a touch of her old tartness.

"Does your cough keep on hurting you jest as much?"

"I don't see's there's much difference."

"Well, I guess I'll get the doctor to come round again," Ann Eliza said, trying for the matter-of-course tone in which one might speak of sending for the plumber or the gas-fitter.

"It ain't any use sending for the doctor—and who's going to pay him?"

"I am," answered the elder sister. "Here's your tea, and a mite of toast. Don't that tempt you?"

Already, in the watches of the night, Ann Eliza had been tormented by that same question—who was to pay the doctor?—and a few days before she had temporarily silenced it by borrowing twenty dollars of Miss Mellins. The transaction had cost her one of the bitterest struggles of her life. She had never borrowed a penny of any one before, and the possibility of having to do so had always been classed in her mind among those shameful extremities to which Providence does not let decent people come. But nowadays she no longer believed in the personal supervision of Providence; and had she been compelled to steal the money instead of borrowing it, she would have felt that her conscience was the only tribunal before which she had to answer. Nevertheless, the actual humiliation of having to ask for the money was no less bitter; and she could hardly hope that Miss Mellins would view the case with the same detachment as herself. Miss Mellins was very kind; but she not unnaturally felt that her kindness should be rewarded by according her the right to ask questions; and bit by bit Ann Eliza saw Evelina's miserable secret slipping into the dress-maker's possession.

When the doctor came she left him alone with Evelina, busying herself in the shop that she might have an opportunity of seeing him alone on his way out. To steady herself she began to sort a trayful of buttons, and when the doctor appeared she was reciting under her breath: "Twenty-four horn, two and a half cards fancy pearl..." She saw at once that his look was grave.

He sat down on the chair beside the counter, and her mind travelled miles before he spoke.

"Miss Bunner, the best thing you can do is to let me get a bed for your sister at St. Luke's."

"The hospital?"

"Come now, you're above that sort of prejudice, aren't you?" The doctor spoke in the tone of one who coaxes a spoiled child. "I know how devoted you are—but Mrs. Ramy can be much better cared for there than here. You really haven't time to look after her and attend to your business as well. There'll be no expense, you understand—"

Ann Eliza made no answer. "You think my sister's going to be sick a good while, then?" she asked.

"Well, yes—possibly."

"You think she's very sick?"

"Well, yes. She's very sick."

His face had grown still graver; he sat there as though he had never known what it was to hurry.

Ann Eliza continued to separate the pearl and horn buttons. Suddenly she lifted her eyes and looked at him. "Is she going to die?"

The doctor laid a kindly hand on hers. "We never say that, Miss Bunner. Human skill works wonders—and at the hospital Mrs. Ramy would have every chance."

"What is it? What's she dying of?"

The doctor hesitated, seeking to substitute a popular phrase for the scientific terminology which rose to his lips.

"I want to know," Ann Eliza persisted.

"Yes, of course; I understand. Well, your sister has had a hard time lately, and there is a complication of causes, resulting in consumption—rapid consumption. At the hospital—"

"I'll keep her here," said Ann Eliza quietly.

After the doctor had gone she went on for some time sorting the buttons; then she slipped the tray into its place on a shelf behind the counter and went into the back room. She found Evelina propped upright against the pillows, a flush of agitation on her cheeks. Ann Eliza pulled up the shawl which had slipped from her sister's shoulders.

"How long you've been! What's he been saying?"

"Oh, he went long ago—he on'y stopped to give me a prescription. I was sorting out that tray of buttons. Miss Mellins's girl got them all mixed up."

She felt Evelina's eyes upon her.

"He must have said something: what was it?"

"Why, he said you'd have to be careful—and stay in bed—and take this new medicine he's given you."

"Did he say I was going to get well?"

"Why, Evelina!"

"What's the use, Ann Eliza? You can't deceive me. I've just been up to look at myself in the glass; and I saw plenty of 'em in the hospital that looked like me. They didn't get well, and I ain't going to." Her head dropped back. "It don't much matter—I'm about tired. On'y there's one thing—Ann Eliza—"

The elder sister drew near to the bed.

"There's one thing I ain't told you. I didn't want to tell you yet because I was afraid you might be sorry—but if he says I'm going to die I've got to say it." She stopped to cough, and to Ann Eliza it now seemed as though every cough struck a minute from the hours remaining to her.

"Don't talk now—you're tired."

"I'll be tireder to-morrow, I guess. And I want you should know. Sit down close to me—there."

Ann Eliza sat down in silence, stroking her shrunken hand.

"I'm a Roman Catholic, Ann Eliza."

"Evelina—oh, Evelina Bunner! A Roman Catholic—*you*? Oh, Evelina, did *he* make you?"

Evelina shook her head. "I guess he didn't have no religion; he never spoke of it. But you see Mrs. Hochmuller was a Catholic, and so when I was sick she got the doctor to send me to a Roman Catholic hospital, and the sisters was so good to me there—and the priest used to come and talk to me; and the things he said kep' me from going crazy. He seemed to make everything easier."

"Oh, sister, how could you?" Ann Eliza wailed. She knew little of the Catholic religion except that "Papists" believed in it—in itself a sufficient indictment. Her spiritual rebellion had not freed her from the formal part of her religious belief, and apostasy had always seemed to her one of the sins from which the pure in mind avert their thoughts.

"And then when the baby was born," Evelina continued, "he christened it right away, so it could go to heaven; and after that, you see, I had to be a Catholic."

"I don't see—"

"Don't I have to be where the baby is? I couldn't ever ha' gone there if I hadn't been made a Catholic. Don't you understand that?"

Ann Eliza sat speechless, drawing her hand away. Once more she found herself shut out of Evelina's heart, an exile from her closest affections.

"I've got to go where the baby is," Evelina feverishly insisted.

Ann Eliza could think of nothing to say; she could only feel that Evelina was dying, and dying as a stranger in her arms. Ramy and the day-old baby had parted her forever from her sister.

Evelina began again. "If I get worse I want you to send for a priest. Miss Mellins'll know where to send—she's got an aunt that's a Catholic. Promise me faithful you will."

"I promise," said Ann Eliza.

After that they spoke no more of the matter; but Ann Eliza now understood that the little black bag about her sister's neck, which she had innocently taken for a memento of Ramy, was some kind of sacrilegious amulet, and her fingers shrank from its contact when she bathed and dressed Evelina. It seemed to her the diabolical instrument of their estrangement.

CHAPTER XIII

Spring had really come at last. There were leaves on the ailanthus-tree that Evelina could see from her bed, gentle clouds floated over it in the blue, and now and then the cry of a flower-seller sounded from the street.

One day there was a shy knock on the back-room door, and Johnny Hawkins came in with two yellow jonquils in his fist. He was getting bigger and squarer, and his round freckled face was growing into a smaller copy of his father's. He walked up to Evelina and held out the flowers.

"They blew off the cart and the fellow said I could keep 'em. But you can have 'em," he announced.

Ann Eliza rose from her seat at the sewing-machine and tried to take the flowers from him.

"They ain't for you; they're for her," he sturdily objected; and Evelina held out her hand for the jonquils.

After Johnny had gone she lay and looked at them without speaking. Ann Eliza, who had gone back to the machine, bent her head over the seam she was stitching; the click, click, click of the machine sounded in her ear like the tick of Ramy's clock, and it seemed to her that life had gone backward, and that Evelina, radiant and foolish, had just come into the room with the yellow flowers in her hand.

When at last she ventured to look up, she saw that her sister's head had drooped against the pillow, and that she was sleeping quietly. Her relaxed hand still held the jonquils, but it was evident that they had awakened no memories; she had dozed off almost as soon as Johnny had given them to her. The discovery gave Ann Eliza a startled sense of the ruins that must be piled upon her past. "I don't believe I could have forgotten that day, though," she said to herself. But she was glad that Evelina had forgotten.

Evelina's disease moved on along the usual course, now lifting her on a brief wave of elation, now sinking her to new depths of weakness. There was little to be done, and the doctor came only at lengthening intervals. On his way out he always repeated his first friendly suggestion about sending Evelina to the hospital; and Ann Eliza always answered: "I guess we can manage."

The hours passed for her with the fierce rapidity that great joy or anguish lends them. She went through the days with a sternly smiling precision, but she hardly knew what was happening, and when night-fall released her from the shop, and she could carry her work to Evelina's bedside, the same sense of unreality accompanied her, and she still seemed to be accomplishing a task whose object had escaped her memory.

Once, when Evelina felt better, she expressed a desire to make some artificial flowers, and Ann Eliza, deluded by this awakening interest, got out the faded bundles of stems and petals and the little tools and spools of wire. But after a few minutes the work dropped from Evelina's hands and she said: "I'll wait until to-morrow."

She never again spoke of the flower-making, but one day, after watching Ann Eliza's laboured attempt to trim a spring hat for Mrs. Hawkins, she demanded impatiently that the hat should be brought to her, and in a trice had galvanized the lifeless bow and given the brim the twist it needed.

These were rare gleams; and more frequent were the days of speechless lassitude, when she lay for hours silently staring at the window, shaken only by the hard incessant cough that sounded to Ann Eliza like the hammering of nails into a coffin.

At length one morning Ann Eliza, starting up from the mattress at the foot of the bed, hastily called Miss Mellins down, and ran through the smoky dawn for the doctor. He came back with her and did what he could to give Evelina momentary relief; then he went away, promising to look in again before night. Miss Mellins, her head still covered with curl-papers, disappeared in his wake, and when the sisters were alone Evelina beckoned to Ann Eliza.

"You promised," she whispered, grasping her sister's arm; and Ann Eliza understood. She had not yet dared to tell Miss Mellins of Evelina's change of faith; it had seemed even more difficult than borrowing the money; but now it had to be done. She ran upstairs after the dress-maker and detained her on the landing.

"Miss Mellins, can you tell me where to send for a priest—a Roman Catholic priest?"

"A priest, Miss Bunner?"

"Yes. My sister became a Roman Catholic while she was away. They were kind to her in her sickness—and now she wants a priest." Ann Eliza faced Miss Mellins with unflinching eyes.

"My aunt Dugan'll know. I'll run right round to her the minute I get my papers off," the dress-maker promised; and Ann Eliza thanked her.

An hour or two later the priest appeared. Ann Eliza, who was watching, saw him coming down the steps to the shop-door and went to meet him. His expression was kind, but she shrank from his peculiar dress, and from his pale face with its bluish chin and enigmatic smile. Ann Eliza remained in the shop. Miss Mellins's girl had mixed the buttons again and she set herself to sort them. The priest stayed a long time with Evelina. When he again carried his enigmatic smile past the counter, and Ann Eliza rejoined her sister, Evelina was smiling with something of the same mystery; but she did not tell her secret.

After that it seemed to Ann Eliza that the shop and the back room no longer belonged to her. It was as though she were there on sufferance, indulgently tolerated by the unseen power which hovered over Evelina even in the absence of its minister. The priest came almost daily; and at last a day arrived when he was called to administer some rite of which Ann Eliza but dimly grasped the sacramental meaning. All she knew was that it meant that Evelina was going, and going, under this alien guidance, even farther from her than to the dark places of death.

When the priest came, with something covered in his hands, she crept into the shop, closing the door of the back room to leave him alone with Evelina.

It was a warm afternoon in May, and the crooked ailanthus-tree rooted in a fissure of the opposite pavement was a fountain of tender green. Women in light dresses passed with the languid step of spring; and presently there came a man with a hand-cart full of pansy and geranium plants who stopped outside the window, signalling to Ann Eliza to buy.

An hour went by before the door of the back room opened and the priest reappeared with that mysterious covered something in his hands. Ann Eliza had risen, drawing back as he passed. He had doubtless divined her antipathy, for he had hitherto only bowed in going in and out; but to day he paused and looked at her compassionately.

"I have left your sister in a very beautiful state of mind," he said in a low voice like a woman's. "She is full of spiritual consolation."

Ann Eliza was silent, and he bowed and went out. She hastened back to Evelina's bed, and knelt down beside it. Evelina's eyes were very large and bright; she turned them on Ann Eliza with a look of inner illumination.

"I shall see the baby," she said; then her eyelids fell and she dozed.

The doctor came again at nightfall, administering some last palliatives; and after he had gone Ann Eliza, refusing to have her vigil shared by Miss Mellins or Mrs. Hawkins, sat down to keep watch alone.

It was a very quiet night. Evelina never spoke or opened her eyes, but in the still hour before dawn Ann Eliza saw that the restless hand outside the bed-clothes had stopped its twitching. She stooped over and felt no breath on her sister's lips.

The funeral took place three days later. Evelina was buried in Calvary Cemetery, the priest assuming the whole care of the necessary arrangements, while Ann Eliza, a passive spectator, beheld with stony indifference this last negation of her past.

A week afterward she stood in her bonnet and mantle in the doorway of the little shop. Its whole aspect had changed. Counter and shelves were bare, the window was stripped of its familiar miscellany of artificial flowers, note-paper, wire hat-frames, and limp garments from the dyer's; and against the glass pane of the doorway hung a sign: "This store to let."

Ann Eliza turned her eyes from the sign as she went out and locked the door behind her. Evelina's funeral had been very expensive, and Ann Eliza, having sold her stock-in-trade and the few articles of furniture that remained to her, was leaving the shop for the last time. She had not been able to buy any mourning, but Miss Mellins had sewed some crape on her old black mantle and bonnet, and having no gloves she slipped her bare hands under the folds of the mantle.

It was a beautiful morning, and the air was full of a warm sunshine that had coaxed open nearly every window in the street, and summoned to the window-sills the sickly plants nurtured indoors in winter. Ann Eliza's way lay westward, toward Broadway; but at the corner she paused and looked back down the familiar length of the street. Her eyes rested a moment on the blotched "Bunner Sisters" above the empty window of the shop; then they travelled on to the overflowing foliage of the Square, above which was the church tower with the dial that had marked the hours for the sisters before Ann Eliza had bought the nickel clock. She looked at it all as though it had been the scene of some unknown life, of which the vague report had reached her: she felt for herself the only remote pity that busy people accord to the misfortunes which come to them by hearsay.

She walked to Broadway and down to the office of the house-agent to whom she had entrusted the sub-letting of the shop. She left the key with one of his clerks, who took it from her as if it had been any one of a thousand others, and remarked that the weather looked as if spring was really coming; then she turned and began to move up the great thoroughfare, which was just beginning to wake to its multitudinous activities.

She walked less rapidly now, studying each shop window as she passed, but not with the desultory eye of enjoyment: the watchful fixity of her gaze overlooked everything but the object of its quest. At length she stopped before a small window wedged between two mammoth buildings, and displaying, behind its shining plate-glass festooned with muslin, a varied assortment of sofa-cushions, tea-cloths, pen-wipers, painted calendars and other specimens of feminine industry. In a corner of the window she had read, on a slip of paper pasted against the pane: "Wanted, a Saleslady," and after studying the display of fancy articles beneath it, she gave her mantle a twitch, straightened her shoulders and went in.

Behind a counter crowded with pin-cushions, watch-holders and other needlework trifles, a plump young woman with smooth hair sat sewing bows of ribbon on a scrap basket. The little shop was about the size of the one on which Ann Eliza had just closed the door; and it looked as fresh and gay and thriving as she and Evelina had once dreamed of making Bunner Sisters. The friendly air of the place made her pluck up courage to speak.

"Saleslady? Yes, we do want one. Have you any one to recommend?" the young woman asked, not unkindly.

Ann Eliza hesitated, disconcerted by the unexpected question; and the other, cocking her head on one side to study the effect of the bow she had just sewed on the basket, continued: "We can't afford more than thirty dollars a month, but the work is light. She would be expected to do a little fancy sewing between times. We want a bright girl: stylish, and pleasant manners. You know what I mean. Not over thirty, anyhow; and nice-looking. Will you write down the name?"

Ann Eliza looked at her confusedly. She opened her lips to explain, and then, without speaking, turned toward the crisply-curtained door.

"Ain't you going to leave the *ad*-dress?" the young woman called out after her. Ann Eliza went out into the thronged street. The great city, under the fair spring sky, seemed to throb with the stir of innumerable beginnings. She walked on, looking for another shop window with a sign in it.

❒❒❒